THE MIDWIFE'S PREGNANCY MIRACLE

BY
KATE HARDY

MILLS & BOON

First published in Great Britain 2016
By Mills & Boon, an imprint of HarperCollins*Publishers*
1 London Bridge Street, London, SE1 9GF

Large Print edition 2017

© 2016 Harlequin Books S.A.

Special thanks and acknowledgement are given to
Kate Hardy for her contribution to the Christmas Miracles
in Maternity series

ISBN: 978-0-263-06696-8

Christmas Miracles in Maternity

*Hope, magic and precious new beginnings
at Teddy's!*

Welcome to Teddy's Centre for Babies and
Birth, where the brightest stars of neonatal
and obstetric medicine work tirelessly to
save tiny lives and deliver bundles of joy all
year round—but there's never a time quite as
magical as Christmas!

Although the temperature might be
dropping outside, unexpected surprises
are heating up for these dedicated pros! And
as Christmas Day draws near secrets are
revealed, hope is ignited and love takes over.

Cuddle up this Christmas with the
heart-warming stories of the doctors, nurses,
midwives and surgeons at Teddy's in the
Christmas Miracles in Maternity mini-series:

Available November 2016

The Nurse's Christmas Gift
by Tina Beckett

The Midwife's Pregnancy Miracle
by Kate Hardy

Available December 2016

White Christmas for the Single Mum
by Susanne Hampton

A Royal Baby for Christmas
by Scarlet Wilson

Dear Reader,

This book is all about a Christmas miracle.

Ella struggled against the odds to become a midwife, and then discovered that it was almost impossible for her to have a baby. Oliver was badly hurt by a previous partner who took away something precious. Neither of them is prepared to have a serious relationship, and they bury themselves in work, suppressing how they really feel about each other.

But one unexpected night leads to an even more unexpected consequence.

And they discover that miracles really do happen.

I hope you enjoy their journey!

With love,

Kate Hardy

Kate Hardy has always loved books, and could read before she went to school. She discovered Mills & Boon books when she was twelve and decided this was what she wanted to do. When she isn't writing Kate enjoys reading, cinema, ballroom dancing and the gym. You can contact her via her website: katehardy.com.

Books by Kate Hardy

Mills & Boon Medical Romance

Her Real Family Christmas
200 Harley Street: The Soldier Prince
It Started with No Strings…
A Baby to Heal Their Hearts
A Promise…to a Proposal?
Her Playboy's Proposal
Capturing the Single Dad's Heart

Mills & Boon Cherish

Falling for Mr December
Billionaire, Boss…Bridegroom?
Holiday with the Best Man

Visit the Author Profile page
at millsandboon.co.uk for more titles.

For Scarlet, Susanne and Tina—really enjoyed
working with you all on our quartet!

Praise for
Kate Hardy

'This was a truly stunning, heartfelt read
from Kate Hardy. She blew me away with the
intensity of the heartache in this read.'
—*Contemporary Romance Reviews* on
The Brooding Doc's Redemption

'*Bound by a Baby* moved me to tears many
times. It is a full-on emotional drama. Author
Kate Hardy brought this tale shimmering with
emotions. Highly recommended for all lovers
of romance.'
—*Contemporary Romance Reviews*

***Bound by a Baby* won the 2014 RoNA
(Romantic Novelists' Association) award!**

PROLOGUE

Hallowe'en

ALMOST AS IF someone had called his name, Oliver Darrington found himself turning round and looking at the doorway.

Ella O'Brien, one of the junior midwives from his department, was standing there. Despite the fact that she was wearing a mask that covered half her face—because tonight was the annual Hallowe'en Masquerade Ball, the glitziest fund-raiser in the Royal Cheltenham Hospital's social calendar—he recognised her instantly.

Desire shimmered at the bottom of his spine and he dragged in a breath. He really needed to get a grip. Ella was his colleague. His friend. He'd been attracted to her since the very first moment she'd walked into Teddy's, the centre for birth and babies at the Royal Cheltenham Hospital. Her striking red hair, worn tied back in a scrunchie, had snagged his attention. Then he'd noticed her clear green eyes and the soft curve of her mouth. He'd wanted her immediately, though he'd held himself back. Since the fallout from dating Justine, Oliver didn't do serious relationships; plus he hadn't wanted to risk making things awkward on the ward between them, so he'd managed to keep things strictly professional between himself and Ella.

Though several times when they'd worked together, his hand had brushed against hers and it had felt as if he'd been galvanised. And sometimes he'd caught her eye and wondered, did she ever feel that same secret pull?

Though he'd dismissed it: Ella O'Brien was one of the most grounded and independent women he'd ever met. He knew she was dedicated to her career and she wasn't the type to let herself be distracted by a fling—which was all he could offer. Besides, over the last eighteen months, he'd discovered that he liked Ella: she was easy to work with, being both sharply intelligent and yet able to empathise with the mums on the unit. He didn't want to risk spoiling that.

But tonight…

Tonight was the first time he'd ever seen her all dressed up, and it threw him. At work, Ella wore uniform or scrubs, and on team nights out she'd always dressed casually in jeans and a T-shirt. Oliver couldn't quite square the no-nonsense midwife he was used to with the woman in the navy satin prom dress. Her dress had a sweetheart neckline and was drawn in sharply at the waist to highlight her curves before flaring out again to the knee, and she was wearing high heels which made her legs look incredibly long. She looked utterly gorgeous. Right at that moment, Oliver really wanted to pull her into his arms and kiss her until they were both dizzy.

'Stop being so shallow, Darrington,' he chided himself.

And then he realised that Ella had hesitated in the doorway; she was clearly scanning the room, trying to work out where the rest of the team was. For just a moment, she looked vulnerable— which was odd for someone who was always so confident and cheerful at work. And that look of uncertainty made him go straight to her rescue.

'Good evening, Ella. You look lovely,' he said as he joined her in the doorway.

Her fair Irish skin turned a delicate shade of pink. 'Thank you, Oliver. But you're not supposed to recognise me with a mask on, are you?'

'Your hair's a tiny bit of a giveaway.' That glorious dark red. And tonight it was in a sophisticated updo, with a few loose, soft curls framing her face, making him want to release the pins and let it fall like silk onto her shoulders... Oh, for pity's sake. Now was definitely not the time to start fantasising about her. He forced himself to concentrate. 'So how did you recognise me?' he asked.

'Your voice is pretty distinctive.'

As was hers, with that soft Irish accent. 'Fair cop,' he said easily. 'The rest of the team from Teddy's is over there.' He gestured in the direction of their table. 'Come and have a glass of champagne.'

Even though Oliver was a good six inches taller than she was, Ella noticed that he kept his stride short to match hers as they skirted round the edge of the dance floor. She was really grateful; the last thing she wanted to do was to make a fool of herself by walking too fast and tripping over in her unfamiliar high heels. Especially here, at such a glamorous do. Right now, she felt seriously out of her depth. She'd never really been much of a one for parties and balls; at university, she'd missed out on most of the big events, because she'd been concentrating so hard on her studies. It had been such a struggle to get to university in the first place, she hadn't wanted to jeopardise her career by partying when she should've been studying. And it was one of the reasons why she was still a virgin at the age of twenty-six: she'd concentrated on her studies rather than on serious relationships. Part of her felt ridiculously self-conscious about it; in this day and age, it was so old-fashioned to still be a virgin. Yet, at the same time, she felt that sex ought to mean something. She didn't want to have a one-night stand with someone just for the sake of it.

Last year, she'd been on duty so she hadn't been able to make it to the famous Royal Cheltenham Masquerade Ball; this year, she was off duty so she didn't have a good excuse to avoid it. But either Oliver hadn't noticed that she was a bit flustered, or he was too sensitive to make an issue of it. He simply chatted to her as they crossed the dance floor to join the rest of the team.

Ella, you look lovely.

Typical Oliver: charming and kind. It was one of the skills that made him popular to work with on the ward, because he always managed to make their mums-to-be feel more at ease and stop worrying. Just as he was clearly trying to put her at her ease now.

Ella had worked with the consultant for the last eighteen months; although she'd been instantly attracted to him, she'd been very careful not to act on that attraction. Although there had been moments when they'd accidentally touched at work and it had made her feel as if her heart was doing a backward flip, and sometimes she'd caught his eye in an unguarded moment and wondered if he felt that same pull, she hadn't acted on it because Oliver Darrington was way, way out of her league. According to the hospital grapevine, the string of women he dated all looked like models or had aristocratic connections; no way would he be interested in a junior midwife who came from a very ordinary family in County Kerry. So she'd kept things strictly professional between them at work, not even confessing to her best friend Annabelle how much she liked Oliver.

And she'd be strictly professional tonight, too.

Which was a real effort, given how gorgeous Oliver looked right now. He usually wore a suit to work, but she'd never seen him wearing evening dress before. He reminded her of Henry Cavill in his *The Man from U.N.C.L.E.* role: tall and handsome, debonair even, with his dark hair perfectly groomed. Except Oliver's eyes were grey rather than blue, and his mouth was even more beautiful than the actor's...

Get a grip, Ella O'Brien, she told herself, and she managed to smile and say the kind of things everyone expected to hear when she and Oliver joined the rest of the team.

The warmth of their welcome dispelled the remainder of her nerves, and she found herself chatting easily.

'Dance with me?' Oliver asked.

This was the stuff dreams were made of: waltzing around a posh ballroom with Oliver Darrington.

Except Ella couldn't dance. She'd always been horribly clumsy. The only thing that she was worse at than dancing was spelling, thanks to her dyslexia. And she'd spent so many years as a child believing that she was stupid and slow and hopeless at everything that she didn't trust herself not to make a mess of dancing with Oliver.

'I should warn you that I have two left feet,' she said. 'And I've never danced to this sort of music.' She gestured to the jazz trio on the stage. 'I've only ever watched *Strictly Come Dancing* on the telly. So on your head—or toes—be it, if you *really* want me to dance with you. But now's your chance to escape with all your toes unbruised.'

'You won't bruise my toes.' He smiled. 'Just follow my lead and it'll be fine.'

Was it really going to be that easy? Ella didn't share his confidence. At all.

But then Oliver led her onto the dance floor and they actually started dancing together.

It felt like floating on air. The way he guided her meant that she was moving in the right direction and her feet were always in the right place. And she'd never, ever experienced anything so magical. It was even better than she'd dreamed. Right at that second she felt like a fairy-tale princess in her swishy-skirted dress, dancing with the handsome prince. And she loved every moment of it. Being in his arms felt so right—as if this was where she'd always belonged. It made her feel warm and safe and cherished; yet, at the same time, there was the slow, sensual burn of attraction, dangerous and exciting.

Oliver danced with her for three songs in a row; and she was greedy enough to want to dance with him all night. Except this was the hospital's charity ball and Oliver was a consultant. He should be mixing, like the rest of the senior staff.

'Shouldn't you be—well—dancing with someone else?' Ella asked, feeling guilty both for being selfish and for wanting Oliver all to herself.

His eyes glittered behind his mask. 'No. It's up to me to decide who I dance with—and I want to dance with you.'

Her heart skipped a beat. Was Oliver telling her that he'd noticed her, the way she'd noticed him over the last few months? That for him, too, this had been building up for a long time? Or was she misreading him and hoping for too much?

'Though would you rather be dancing with someone else?' he asked.

'No, no—not at all.' Though she rather thought that Oliver might have spoiled her for dancing with anyone else, ever again. Not that she was going to admit that to him.

'Good.' He kept her in his arms, and Ella's pulse went up a notch as they moved round the dance floor.

Oliver knew he shouldn't be doing this. He'd meant to dance with Ella once, to be polite and friendly, then keep his distance.

The problem was, he really liked the feel of her in his arms. Which again was ridiculous, because Oliver didn't do proper relationships. Not since Justine. He was well aware that the hospital grapevine had labelled him a heartbreaker, a playboy who had an endless string of one-night stands. There was a grain of truth in the rumours, because he never got involved with anyone for the long term; but he really wasn't a heartbreaker and he was picky about who he slept with. He always made sure that every woman he dated knew the score right from the start: that it was just for fun, just for now and not for always. He definitely didn't leave a trail of broken hearts behind him, because that would be unkind and unfair.

But there was something about Ella that drew him. A simplicity of heart, maybe?

Which was precisely why he ought to make an excuse and get her to dance with someone else. Put some space between them until his common sense came back. He didn't want to mess up their working relationship. Even though right now he really, really wanted to dance her into a quiet corridor and kiss her until they were both dizzy.

Then he became aware that she was speaking and shook himself. 'Sorry, Ella. I was wool-gathering. What did you say?'

She gave him the sweetest, sweetest smile— one that made his heart feel as if it had just turned over. 'Nothing important.'

'I guess I ought to stop monopolising you and let you dance with someone else,' he said.

Which was Oliver being nice and taking the blame for her social mistakes, Ella thought. 'Yes,' she agreed. She kept the bright smile pinned on her face as they went back to join the rest of the team. Then Charlie Warren, one of the other doctors from Teddy's, asked her to dance. Although Charlie was usually quite reserved, his offer was genuine enough, so she accepted.

'So are you enjoying the ball, Ella, or here under sufferance like me?' Charlie asked.

'I'm enjoying myself.' In fact, much more than she'd expected to. Though she had a nasty feeling that Oliver was the main reason for that. 'I'm sorry you're not.'

'I never do, really,' Charlie began, then grimaced when she trod on his toes.

'Sorry,' she said instantly. 'I'm afraid I have two left feet.'

'I thought all Irish people were supposed to be natural dancers? I guess you have *Riverdance* to blame for that.' It was an attempt at humour, as he was obviously trying to make polite conversation, but for as long as Ella had known Charlie, he'd always been distant with everyone at work. Quite the lone wolf.

'Sadly, that gene bypassed me,' she said. 'I'm more Flatfeet than Flatley.'

'I think my toes have already worked that one out for themselves but, even though we're no Fred

Astaire and Ginger Rogers, you look lovely to-night, Ella.'

'Thank you,' she said smiling. 'I think you look more like James Bond than Fred Astaire anyway.'

'You're very sweet, Ella.' He gave her a shy half-smile. 'And you've made an otherwise dull evening much nicer.'

Ella found herself going through a similar routine with the colleagues she danced with from the Emergency Department.

'You know, we're going to have to set up a special broken toe department in the unit, just for the men you've danced with tonight,' Mike Wetherby teased.

'So I'd be better off sticking to delivering babies than dancing, hmm?' she teased back, knowing that he meant no harm by the comment.

'You can dance with me any time you like, Ella O'Brien,' Mike said. 'As long as I have fair warning so I can put on my steel-toe-capped boots first.'

She just laughed. 'In steel-toe-capped boots, you'd be clomping around the dance floor as badly as me.'

'Then we'd be the perfect match.'

'Yeah, yeah.'

And then Oliver rested his hand on Ella's shoulder. 'The next dance is mine, I believe.'

The warmth of his fingers against her bare skin sent a shaft of pure desire through her. She reminded herself crossly that this was a charity ball and Oliver had danced with at least half a dozen other women. He'd treated them in just the same way that he'd treated her, with courtesy and gallantry, so she was kidding herself and setting herself up for disappointment if she thought that his behaviour towards her tonight was anything more than that of a colleague. And she wasn't going to embarrass herself by throwing herself at him and being turned down.

Was it wishful thinking or did the lights actually dim slightly as they moved onto the dance floor?

Oliver drew her closer, and she shivered.

'Cold?' he asked.

'No, I'm fine,' she said, not wanting him to guess that her reaction had been something so very different.

He pulled back slightly and looked her in the eye. For a second, Ella could've sworn that the same deep, intense yearning she felt was re-flected in his eyes. But that had to be imagina-tion or wishful thinking. Of course he didn't feel like that about her. Why would he?

She stared at his mouth, wondering for a crazy second what it would be like if Oliver kissed her. It must be that second glass of champagne affect-ing her, she thought, vowing to stick to water for the rest of the evening.

But dancing with Oliver was headier than any amount of champagne. And she noticed that, al-though she'd been clumsy with her other part-ners, with Oliver she didn't seem to put a foot wrong. Dancing with him made her feel as if someone had put a spell on her—but a nice spell, one that made her feel good.

And when he drew her closer still, she rested her head on his shoulder and closed her eyes. Just for these few moments, she could believe that she and Oliver were together. Just the two of them, dancing cheek to cheek, with nobody else in the room. Just them and the night and the music…

At the end of the evening, Oliver said casually, 'I think you're on my way home, Ella. Can I give you a lift?'

The sensible thing to do would be to smile politely and say thanks, but she'd be fine—though she hadn't remembered to book a taxi, and there was bound to be an enormous queue so she'd have to wait for ages in the cold. It was a twenty-minute drive from here to her flat. She could manage that without making a fool of herself and throwing herself at Oliver, couldn't she?

'Thank you. That's very kind of you,' she said. 'It'll save me having to wait ages for a taxi.'

'Pleasure,' he said. 'Shall we go?'

She walked with him to his car. It was icy outside, and the thin wrap she'd brought did nothing to protect her from the cold.

'Here,' he said, shrugging out of his jacket and sliding it across her shoulders.

'But you'll be cold,' she protested.

'Not as cold as you,' he said.

Typical Oliver: gallant and charming. But she appreciated the warmth of his jacket, and tried not to think about the fact that it had been warmed by Oliver's body heat.

Just as she'd half expected, his car was sleek and low-slung. When he opened the door for her,

Ella nearly tripped getting in and was cross with herself for being so stupid and clumsy.

'Ella, relax. There aren't any strings. This is just a lift home,' he said.

More was the pity, she thought, and was even crosser with herself for being such an idiot.

'Sorry. Too much champagne,' she fibbed.

When she fumbled with the seat belt, he sorted it out for her. Her skin tingled where his fingers brushed against her.

Stop it, she told herself. He doesn't think of you in *that* way. And you're too busy at work to get involved with anyone—especially a colleague who apparently never dates anyone more than twice. Keep it professional.

'What's your postcode?' he asked.

She told him and he put it into the sat nav. Then he switched on the stereo and soft classical music flooded the car. 'Do you mind this?' he asked. 'I can change it, if you like.'

'No, it's lovely. I like piano music,' she said. 'We have a piano at home.'

'You play?'

'No, Mam does. I meant home in Ireland, not here,' she said. 'Mam's a music teacher. She plays

the piano at school in assembly and in the Christmas Nativity plays for the little ones.'

'Did you ever think about being a teacher?' he
asked.

'No.' Everyone had thought that little Ella
O'Brien was very sweet but not very bright, and
would never get through her exams. Until the new
biology teacher had started at her school when
Ella was fifteen, worked out that Ella was dyslexic rather than stupid, and batted her corner
for her. 'I always wanted to be a midwife, like
my Aunty Bridget.' Everyone had thought that
Ella was being a dreamer when she'd said what
she wanted to do, but she'd put in the effort and
worked so hard that she'd managed to get through
her exams with good enough grades to get a place
in London to train as a midwife. 'It's so special,
sharing those first few minutes of a new life coming into the world.' She paused. 'What about you?
Did you always want to be a doctor?'

'Yes.' Though there was something slightly
shuttered in Oliver's voice, and Ella wondered
if he'd had the same kind of struggle she'd had
about her choice of career. Although her parents
supported her now, they'd worried throughout

the whole of her degree and her training as a midwife, even though her tutors knew about her dyslexia and were really supportive. Her parents had told her all the time that she ought to give it up and come home to Ireland—particularly when she'd had her operation for a ruptured ovarian cyst and fallen behind in her studies. Thankfully Ella had been stubborn about it, and her parents had eventually come to terms with the fact that she was staying in England. She tried to make it home for a visit every couple of months, as well as video-calling them at least once a week through her laptop. And nowadays she knew her parents were more proud of her than worried about her.

Oliver didn't elaborate on his comment, and she felt too awkward to ask anything more. Particularly as she was so physically aware of him sitting next to her.

Well, she was just going to have to be sensible about this. But, when he pulled up on the road outside her flat, her mouth clearly wasn't with the programme, because she found herself saying, 'Thank you for the lift. Would you like to come in for a coffee?'

* * *

This was where Oliver knew that he was supposed to say no. Where he was supposed to wish Ella goodnight, wait until she was safely indoors and then drive away. But he discovered that his mouth wasn't working in partnership with his common sense, because he found himself saying yes and following her into her flat.

Her tiny flat was on the ground floor in one of the pretty Regency squares in Cheltenham.

'Come and sit down.' She ushered him into the living room. 'Black, one sugar, isn't it?'

'Yes. Thanks.'

'I'll be two seconds,' she said, and disappeared off to what he presumed was her kitchen.

He glanced around the room. There was enough space for a small sofa, a bookcase full of midwifery texts, and a very compact desk where there were more textbooks and a laptop. It looked as if Ella spent a lot of time outside work studying.

There was a framed photograph on the mantelpiece of her at graduation with two people who looked enough like her to be her parents, plus several others of a large group of people in a garden. Clearly she was at some family party or other, and everyone seemed to radiate love and happiness. Oliver felt a momentary pang. His own family wasn't like that, though perhaps part of that was his own fault for distancing himself from them. He could hardly be close to his brother while avoiding his parents, though; and when he saw his parents he was always on the receiving end of their disappointment.

Sometimes he thought that most parents would've been proud of their son for sticking through fourteen years of training and qualifying as an obstetrician. But the Darringtons had had rather different expectations for their son…

He really ought to make his excuses and leave. Ella was the last person he should get involved with. Apart from the fact that she was obviously much closer to her family than he was to his, she was his colleague and he didn't want things to get messy at work. Nothing could happen between them.

But when he went into her small kitchen to tell her that he needed to go, she turned round and smiled at him and all his common sense fled. Her beautiful green eyes held him spellbound. And right at that moment he felt the strongest connection to her. Her mouth looked warm and sweet and soft, and he really wanted to kiss her. When his gaze flicked up to her eyes again, he realised that she was doing exactly the same: looking at his mouth. So was she, too, wondering...?

Instead of saying goodnight, he stepped forward and brushed his mouth very lightly against hers—just as he'd wanted to do all evening. Not just all evening, if he was honest with himself: he'd wanted to kiss her for weeks and weeks and weeks.

Every nerve-end in his lips tingled, so he couldn't stop himself doing it again.

And this time she kissed him back.

'Ella,' he said when he broke the kiss. 'I've wanted to do that for months.'

'Me, too,' she whispered.

So she'd noticed him in the same way?

His common sense made a last-ditch bid to extract him. 'We shouldn't do this.'

'I know—we work together and we ought to be sensible,' she agreed.

'Exactly,' he said, relieved that he hadn't quite ruined their working relationship by giving in to that mad urge to kiss her. They could still salvage a professional friendship after tonight.

But then she rested her hand against his cheek. Her touch was light and gentle, and he found himself twisting his head to kiss her palm.

Her beautiful green eyes darkened.

Then the kissing started all over again, this time in earnest, and Oliver forgot all his good intentions. He loosened her hair, the way he'd wanted to do all evening, and let it tumble down to her shoulders.

Her eyes widened. 'Oliver!'

'I know.' He kissed her again. 'But I can't help this—I really want you, Ella. I have done since the first time I met you.'

'Me, too,' she said.

His whole body tingled with desire. She wanted him as much as he wanted her?

'So what are we going to do about this?' she asked.

'Right now, I can't think straight,' he admitted. 'I just want to make love with you.'

For a moment, he thought she was going to back away. But then she inclined her head very slightly and took his hand to lead him to her bedroom.

'Are you sure about this?' he asked softly as she switched the bedside light on.

'I'm sure,' she said, her voice low and husky.

He kissed her, and it made his head spin. Hardly able to believe this was happening, he slid the zip down at the back of her dress. Seconds later, he stroked the material away from her shoulders and it fell to the floor.

She undid his bow tie, then unbuttoned his shirt with shaking fingers, smoothed the material off his shoulders and let it fall to the floor next to her dress.

He unsnapped her bra. 'You're beautiful. All curves.'

She gave him a shy smile. 'You're beautiful, too. All muscles.'

And suddenly the faint awkwardness was gone—there was just Ella, kissing her, and feeling the warmth of her skin against his.

Oliver wasn't sure which of them finished undressing whom, but the next thing he knew he was kneeling between her thighs and her hair was spread over the pillows, just as he'd imagined it.

And then he stopped. 'Protection. I don't have a condom.'

'You don't need one,' she said, flushing slightly.

So she was on the Pill? Part of him remembered Justine's treachery and the repercussions. But he knew that Ella wasn't like Justine. The woman he'd got to know over the last eighteen months was open and honest. She wasn't going to cheat on him with someone else, get pregnant, and then try to make him believe that the baby was his. He knew that without having to ask.

'Oliver?' She looked worried, now. 'I don't sleep around. I'm not...' The colour in her cheeks deepened. 'You know.'

'I know.' He stroked her face. 'And the rumours about me aren't true. I don't have sex with every single woman I date.' He shouldn't be having sex with Ella, either; but right now her skin was warm against his, this had been a long time coming, and he wanted to do this more than he'd wanted to do anything in years.

'I know,' she said, and kissed him.

That kiss made him relax with her, and he slowed the pace down, wanting to explore her. He kissed and stroked his way down her body, starting with a dip beneath her collarbones and paying attention to exactly what made her sigh with pleasure, from the curve of her inner elbow to the soft undersides of her breasts, then starting with the hollows of her anklebones and feathering his way upwards until she was making tiny, involuntary noises and clutching at his shoulders.

'Now?' he asked softly.

'Now.' Her voice was raspy and husky with desire. Which was exactly what he'd wanted.

As he eased into her, he felt her tense.

'OK?' he asked.

She nodded. 'I just never thought it would be like...'

Her words slammed into his brain and he realised the implication of what she'd just said.

Ella was a virgin. And he'd just taken her virginity.

Oh, hell. But it was too late now. He couldn't reverse what he'd done. All he could do was try to make this as good for her as he could.

'Oliver?' And now she looked panicky. As if she thought she'd done something wrong.

It wasn't her. He was the one in the wrong. He should've thought. Should've checked. Should've walked away, instead of giving in to that desperate need to be close to her.

'You're beautiful,' he said, staying perfectly still so her body would have the time and space to get used to him, and kissed her. Because then he wouldn't have to talk and make a mess of things.

Slowly, she relaxed again, and kissed him back. And he paid close attention, finding out what made her whimper with desire, taking it slowly until he finally felt her body rippling round his and it tipped him into his own climax.

He held her close. 'Ella. I feel so guilty about this.'

'Don't. You didn't do anything wrong.' She stroked his face.

'But you were a—'

'Virgin. I know.' She bit her lip. 'Which is so stupid in this day and age. It makes me feel... Well, who on earth is still a virgin at the age of twenty-six?' She grimaced.

He knew the answer to that. 'A woman who's waiting for the right person.'

'There's no guarantee that Mr Right will ever come along.'

Or Ms Right. She had a point.

And right now she was clearly embarrassed by the situation, because her fair skin was flushed.

'I'm not judging you,' he said awkwardly. 'Ella, you're lovely.'

The 'but' was a mile high in flashing neon letters, and she obviously saw that straight away. 'But you don't do relationships,' she said. 'I know.'

'I'm sorry. I should go.' He dragged in a breath. 'But at the same time I don't want to leave you. I don't want to leave it messy like this.'

'I'm not expecting anything from you, Oliver.'

But he'd seen the flicker of disappointment in her eyes before she'd managed to hide it. She'd just given him her virginity. To simply walk away from her immediately after that would make him feel like a real lowlife.

Plus he didn't actually want to go. Having Ella in his arms felt so *right*.

'Can I stay for a bit and just—well, hold you?' he asked.

'Why?'

One answer slammed into his head, but he wasn't ready to consider that. He took a deep breath. 'Because I feel horrible. I can't just get up and leave you. I just took your virginity, Ella.'

'That isn't an issue.'

He rather thought it was. 'I feel bad about it.'

'Don't. It was my choice.' She paused. 'But you don't want a relationship with me.'

Trust Ella to hit the nail on the head instead of avoiding the issue. His no-nonsense colleague was back. 'It's not *you*. It's anyone.' He raked a hand through his hair. 'I've got an interview for the Assistant Head of Obstetrics job next week. If I get the post, then all my attention's going to be on my new job. It's the wrong time for me to get involved with anyone.'

'And I'm not your type anyway.'

Actually, she was exactly his type, warm and sweet and lovely; though his family wouldn't agree with him. His brother would be fine, but his parents would see her as the girl from a very different background—an unsuitable background. Not that anyone at work knew about his family. He'd been careful to keep his background very quiet. The fact that his father had a title had absolutely nothing to do with Oliver's ability to do his job, and he wanted people to judge him for himself, not for whose son he was.

He took her hand. 'Ella. I like you a lot. I respect you. And I've been attracted to you ever since the first time I met you. What happened tonight...I think it's been a long time coming.'

'It has.'

So she felt that weird, almost elemental pull, too?

'But we're not going to repeat it.'

He couldn't tell a thing from her expression or from the tone of her voice. Everything was neutral. 'It's not you, Ella. It's me.' The last thing he wanted was for her to take the blame. He knew the whole thing was his fault. He should've kept himself under his usual control.

'As far as everyone else is concerned, you gave me a lift home from the ball—as your colleague—and you stayed for a cup of coffee,' she said. 'And that's it.'

'Thank you.' She really was letting him off the hook—and it was a lot more than he deserved.

'If you, um, need the bathroom, it's next door. The towels are clean. Help yourself to anything you need.'

'Thanks.' He pulled on his underpants and padded to the bathroom.

When he returned from his shower, with the towel still wrapped round his waist, she'd changed into a pair of pyjamas. Totally unsexy striped flannel pyjamas that buttoned right up to the neck.

And how bad was it that he wanted to unbutton them and slide the material off her skin again? To kiss every centimetre of skin he uncovered and lose himself in her warmth?

Then again, those pyjamas were also a statement. She was dressed—and he was wearing only her bath towel. 'Do you want me to go?' he asked.

'I think it would be best,' she said.

He knew she was right, and that leaving would be the sensible thing to do, but he still felt bad. As if he should've stayed a bit longer, and at least held her until she fell asleep. Going now felt as if he was deserting her.

'I'm sorry,' he said.

'I'm not.' She lifted her chin. 'We did nothing to be ashamed of.'

He had. He'd taken her virginity without a second thought. But if he pressed the issue, he had a feeling she'd take it the wrong way and think he was ashamed about sleeping with her—that she was the problem, not him. Which wasn't true.

'Uh-huh,' he said awkwardly. Normally he was

good with words, but tonight that ability had completely deserted him. 'Ella—we've worked together well for eighteen months. I don't want that to change.'

'It won't. Nobody at the hospital needs to know anything about what just happened.'

She didn't meet his eye, he noticed. So that comment about not being ashamed had obviously been sheer bravado.

'I'm not a good bet when it comes to relationships, Ella,' he said softly. Though he didn't want to tell her why. How stupid was he not to have realised that Justine had been seeing someone else, and that he was her golden ticket to the good life for her and the baby that wasn't his? He knew that Ella wasn't a gold-digger, the way Justine had been; but he still couldn't face taking a risk with a relationship again. Making another mistake. Having his heart trampled on again. So it was better to stay exactly as he was, where everyone knew the score and that all his relationships were just for fun.

Not a good bet when it comes to relationships.
Neither am I, Ella thought ruefully.

What did she have to offer anyone? Thanks to the endometriosis that had dogged her for years and caused the ovarian cyst to grow and rupture, Ella couldn't have children. It was one of the reasons why she'd avoided relationships; what was the point of starting anything when you knew you were taking someone's future choices away? Who would want a wife who couldn't give him a family? She'd seen first-hand from her own best friend's experience how the pressure of infertility could cause even the strongest marriage to crack.

So she knew she was better off as she was. She'd come to terms with the situation over the last few years; now she had the chance to concentrate on her job and prove that she was better than her grades at university suggested—that she was worthy of her job. And her job would be enough for her.

'I don't want a relationship with you, Oliver,' she said. It wasn't strictly true, but she wasn't stupid enough to long for something she knew she couldn't have. 'Except a working one.'

The relief in his expression was so dazzling, it almost blinded her.

Well, she could be just as bright and chirpy.

She wasn't going to let him see how much his relief had hurt her. 'Shall I make you a cup of tea while you're getting dressed?'

'No, it's fine, thank you. I'd probably better go.'

'I'll, um, let you get changed,' she said, and headed for the kitchen to give him some space.

The two mugs of instant coffee—never made—sat accusingly in front of the kettle. She tipped the coffee granules in the bin, rinsed out the mugs and made herself a strong cup of tea. Mam's solution to everything, she thought wryly. Though she had a feeling that it would take an awful lot more than a cup of tea to sort this out.

She'd just have to pretend that tonight had never happened. And hopefully things wouldn't be awkward between Oliver and her at work.

CHAPTER ONE

Saturday 3rd December

'EXCUSE ME, PLEASE. I'll be back in a second.'
Ella held her breath and made a dash for the door.
This was hardly professional behaviour, but it
would be better than throwing up in front of the
poor mum-to-be and her partner.

She made it to the staff toilet with seconds to
spare. And then, weirdly, as she leaned over the
bowl, she stopped feeling sick.

Huh?

If she was coming down with the sickness bug
that was sweeping its way through the hospital
and leaving all the departments short-staffed,
she should've been throwing up right now. Big
time. But the queasiness that had left her feeling
hot and sweaty in the consulting room seemed
to have vanished.

She frowned. The last thing she'd been aware

of was how strong the dad-to-be's aftershave had been.

Sensitive to smells and feeling sick...

Had any other woman listed those symptoms, Ella would've suspected early pregnancy. But she knew that she couldn't possibly be pregnant. Her doctor had given her the bad news more than five years ago, after her ovarian cyst had ruptured. Between the cyst and the endometriosis that had dogged Ella and caused her to fall behind in her studies, her Fallopian tubes were in a bad way and she'd been told she'd never have children of her own.

How ironic that she'd specialised in midwifery. Cuddles with a baby she'd just delivered, or with a friend's or cousin's child, were all she would ever have. But after a lot of heartache and tears she'd come to terms with the situation. She loved her job. Trying to find a Mr Right who wouldn't mind that she couldn't ever give him a baby of his own—well, that was just being greedy and expecting too much.

She splashed water on her face, took a deep breath and returned to the consulting room to finish the antenatal appointment with her parents-to-be.

But when exactly the same thing happened at her next antenatal appointment, Ella began to wonder quite what was going on.

She and Oliver hadn't used protection, the night of the Hallowe'en masked ball. But she'd thought it wouldn't matter.

Of course she wasn't pregnant. She couldn't be.

As for the fact that her bra felt a bit too tight and her breasts felt slightly sore... That was purely psychological. Her imagination was simply running riot and coming up with other pregnancy symptoms. There was no way this could be a miracle baby. No way at all.

But, now she thought about it, her period was late. A quick mental count told her that it was two and a half weeks late. She hadn't had time to notice because they'd been so short-staffed and busy in the department lately. Actually, that was probably the reason why her period was late in the first place; she'd been rushed off her feet and working crazy hours, so it wasn't surprising that her menstrual cycle was protesting.

'Ella O'Brien, you're being a numpty,' she told

herself crossly. 'Of course you're not pregnant.' All the same, during her break she took one of the pregnancy test kits from the cupboard. Just to prove to herself once and for all that she was being ridiculous, and then she could get on with the rest of her life.

She peed on the stick, then waited.

A blue line appeared in the first window, to show that the test was working properly.

And then, to her shock, a blue line appeared in the second window.

But—but—this couldn't be happening. It *couldn't*. How could she possibly be pregnant?

She sat there staring at the test, in turmoil, emotions whirling through her.

The test result was clear: she was expecting a baby. The one thing she'd been told would never happen, by specialists she'd trusted absolutely. From what they'd said, the odds were so stacked against her falling pregnant, she'd have more chances of winning a huge prize on the lottery.

Though in some ways this felt better than winning the lottery. A baby. The gift she'd never dreamed she'd ever be able to have, except from the sidelines. Although she'd smiled and been genuinely pleased whenever one of her cousins or one of her friends had announced she was pregnant, a tiny part of Ella had mourned the fact she'd never know the joy of being a mum. And now she was actually going to be a mum. Have a baby of her own. For a moment, sheer joy flooded through her. Despite almost impossible odds, she was going to have a baby. A Christmas miracle.

But then panic took over. What about her career? She'd already lost a lot of ground during her studies, thanks to the combination of her dyslexia and the pain of the endometriosis. Some days, the pain had been so debilitating that she hadn't been able to sit through lectures, and she'd had to borrow notes from friends instead of recording the lectures, and struggled as the words danced across the page. Even when her doctor had finally found some medication to help deal with the pain, things hadn't got much better, because then she'd had the ruptured cyst...

She'd worried that if her tutors knew the truth about her illness, they'd make her drop the course. They knew about her dyslexia and they'd already given her so much help, letting her record lectures so she could listen to them and absorb the knowledge that way. She couldn't possibly ask for yet more help. It'd be greedy and selfish. Ella almost gave in to her parents' suggestion to forget all about being a midwife and go home to Ireland. But then she'd had a work placement and she'd loved working on the ward so much. It had made her more determined to follow her dream of being a midwife, so she'd struggled on and scraped through her exams.

And she was always aware that she should've done better as a student, that her grades had let her down. It drove her to work harder on the ward, to prove to everyone round her that she was better than her exam results said she was. All the way through her medical career, she'd asked to use computer software to dictate notes rather than rely on her terrible handwriting, she'd used coloured lenses in her glasses so she could manage with bright paper or a screen, and she'd asked colleagues to proofread her notes—because she'd never, ever put a patient at risk by not double-checking that everything in the notes was absolutely correct. And, even though people weren't supposed to discriminate against you at work if you had a medical condition, Ella had always felt the need to work extra hard, just to prove that her dyslexia wouldn't make any difference to her ability to do her job.

But going on maternity leave in six months' time would have a huge impact on her career. She'd lose experience and study time. And what would happen when her maternity leave had ended? Juggling work and still managing to spend a decent amount of time with the baby, as a single parent, was going to be tricky. Arranging childcare to fit round her shifts would be tricky, too.

Though she wasn't the baby's only parent.

And that was something else that worried her.

There was only one man who could be the father, because she'd only ever slept with Oliver.

Once.

How, how, *how* had she managed to get pregnant? Then again, how many times had a young mum-to-be cried on her shoulder that it had been the first time she'd had sex and she'd been so sure you couldn't get pregnant if it was your first time?

But, that night, Ella had told Oliver it was safe not to use a condom. Her doctors had been so sure that she couldn't have children—that her Fallopian tubes were so badly damaged that she probably wouldn't be able to have children even with the help of IVF—that she really *had* believed it was safe not to use a condom.

And now here she was: single, and pregnant with Oliver's baby after a one-night stand. How on earth was she going to tell him about the baby?

She had absolutely no idea what Oliver would say or how he'd react to the news. Since the night of the ball, things between them had cooled considerably. She wasn't sure which of the two of them was the more embarrassed about what had happened. He'd really reacted badly once he'd realised that she'd been a virgin. Working together had been awkward, and both of them had made excuses to avoid work social events where the other might be there.

Things had cooled even more when it turned out that Oliver had got the job as Assistant Head of Obstetrics. Although he wasn't directly Ella's boss, he was very much her senior. The last thing she wanted was for him—or anyone else at Teddy's—to think that she'd slept with him in an attempt to boost her career. She'd never do anything like that.

At least Oliver wasn't dating anyone else, as far as she knew, so that was one less complication to worry about. But how did you tell someone that you were expecting his baby, when you weren't even in a relationship with him and you had no idea how he'd react?

She couldn't even begin to frame the right words.

She knew she wasn't going to get a happy-ever-after, where Oliver went down on one knee with a hand clutched to his chest, declared his undying love for her and asked her to marry him. Though she wasn't naive enough to expect that. And if he did ask her, she certainly wasn't going to marry a man who didn't love her, just for the baby's sake. That wouldn't be fair to any of them.

But Ella did want Oliver to be involved with the baby. She'd had a really happy childhood. She'd been an only child, but her parents had both come from big families and she'd had plenty of cousins around, so it had been almost as good as having siblings. She wanted that for her baby, too: that feeling of being loved and wanted, of being part of a family. And, even though she wasn't expecting Oliver to resurrect anything more than a distant kind of friendship with her, she hoped that he would at least be there for their child as the baby grew up. It would be a terrible shame for either of them to miss out on any of that.

But what if Oliver didn't want anything to do with the baby at all? What if he expected her to have a termination?

Then she'd have to rethink her situation at the Royal Cheltenham. Seriously. She already knew that she absolutely didn't want a termination. Though working with Oliver in any way, shape or form would be impossible if he expected her to take that option. She'd have to leave the hospital and find a job somewhere else.

Even though she loved her job here at Teddy's, Ella knew she would need some support with the baby. Even if Oliver didn't expect her to have a termination, if he didn't want to be involved with the baby, then she'd have no choice but to go home to Ireland. Although her parents would be shocked and a bit disappointed in her at first, she knew they loved her and wanted the best for her. And she knew how much they'd wanted to be grandparents, even though they'd assured her that of course they weren't bothered by her infertility. They'd be on her side and help her with the baby, and maybe she could work part-time as a midwife in Limerick. Have the best of both worlds.

She cupped her hands protectively around her abdomen. 'Right at this moment, I have no idea how this is going to work out, baby,' she said softly. 'But one thing I do know: I definitely want you. I never dreamed I'd be lucky enough to have you, and I'm so glad I am. You're the best thing that's ever happened to me—and I'm going to try my hardest to be the best mum to you I can.'

She splashed water on her face, wrapped the test kit in a plastic bag and stored it in her pocket, then returned to the ward.

'Are you all right, Ella?' Annabelle, her best friend and the head neonatal nurse on the ward, asked.

'I'm fine,' Ella fibbed. 'You haven't seen Oliver anywhere, have you?'

'I think he's in a meeting. Is it urgent, or can one of the other doctors fill in for him?'

It wasn't urgent exactly—her pregnancy

wouldn't show for a few weeks yet—but absolutely nobody else could fill in for him on this. Not that she could tell Annabelle without telling her the rest of it. And, given the reasons why Annabelle's marriage to Max had collapsed, Ella wanted to choose her words carefully so she didn't rip open her best friend's old scars. Particularly as Max was now working at Teddy's, easing in to a role as Sienna's maternity cover. Annabelle had opened her heart to Ella about the situation, the previous day, and Ella just couldn't say anything that might hurt her best friend.

'It'll wait,' Ella said, trying to keep her voice light.

And it was probably for the best that Oliver wasn't available right now. It would give her some space and time to think about how she was going to tell him the news.

The afternoon was also filled with antenatal appointments; one mum in particular was really worried.

'So this baby's in the same position that her brother was in?' Sara Reynolds asked.

'Back to back—yes,' Ella confirmed.

'So that means another long labour followed by

an emergency section?' Sara grimaced. 'I know I agreed to a trial of labour, but I'm so scared my scar might come open halfway through and I'll have to be rushed into the operating theatre. And the idea of being in labour for two days again and then being stuck in bed for a week, feeling as bad as I did last time, when Jack's so lively…' She shook her head. 'I can't do it. I can't, Ella.'

'It's not going to be like that,' Ella reassured her. 'We'll keep a really close eye on you, and we're not going to let you struggle. Though you're right about a back-to-back labour taking longer, and this little one's been very happily settled in that position for the last three appointments.'

'You don't think she'll move round?'

'At this stage, no. I'll go and have a word with your consultant,' Ella said, 'but I'm pretty sure he'll agree with me in the circumstances that we should be able to offer you an elective section.'

'But if I have a section, doesn't that mean I'll be stuck in bed for a week and I won't be able to drive for a month?' Sara looked worried. 'And I need the car to get Jack to nursery. It's four miles away and there isn't a bus.'

'Last time,' Ella said gently, 'you'd had a two-day labour before the section. It's not surprising that it took it out of you. This time round, you won't have to go through that first, so it'll be easier and you'll be a lot more mobile. Nowadays we say you can drive when you feel ready, though if you can give it three weeks to let yourself heal that would be good. Maybe one of your family or friends nearby can help with the nursery run?'

Sara bit her lip. 'My cousin said she'd come and help.'

'Well, that's great.' Ella smiled at her and squeezed her hand. 'Give me five minutes and I'll have a chat with your consultant.'

Who *would* have to be Oliver, she saw with dismay as she looked at Sara's notes on the computer screen.

Provided she didn't let herself think about the situation she hadn't had a chance to discuss with him, she should be able to deal with this. Her patient had to come first.

Thankfully, Oliver was out of his meeting. Ella could see him sitting at his computer, typing away and looking slightly grim. Working on notes following his meeting, maybe? Hopefully he wouldn't mind the interruption. She rapped on his open door. 'You look busy, but please can I interrupt you for three minutes on behalf of one of my mums, given that you're her consultant and you need to be the one to sign off on the decisions?'

'Sure.'

He didn't smile at her, but that was OK. This was work. She ran through the brief. 'The mum is Sara Reynolds, thirty-six weeks, second baby. Last time round, the baby was back-to-back and she had a two-day labour followed by an emergency section. This baby's been in the same position for the last three appointments, and I don't think she's going to move now. Sara originally agreed to a trial of labour, but she's really worried that she'll end up with another long labour, and she'll have to have another emergency section that'll leave her unable to function for weeks. Given the baby's position and that Sara's got a really lively toddler to cope with as well, I really think she'd be better off having a planned section.'

'Let me look at her notes so I can bring myself up to speed with exactly what happened last time,' Oliver said.

'OK.' And please don't let him be long, Ella thought. She was starting to pick up the smell from his coffee cup and it was making her stomach roil.

But clearly his computer system was on a go-slow when it came to retrieving the patient's notes, and it got to the point where she couldn't bear the smell of coffee any more.

'Excuse me a moment,' she said, and fled to the toilet. Thankfully it was queasiness again rather than actually being sick, and she splashed water onto her face until she felt able to cope again.

When she got back to Oliver's office, he'd clearly had time to review Sara's notes.

'Are you all right?' he asked.

'Yes. I just felt a bit...' No, now really wasn't the time for her to tell him that it was morning sickness. She stopped. 'I'm fine.'

'If you're going down with that sickness bug, I want you off the ward right now before you pass it on to anyone else,' he said. 'Go home, Ella.'

'It's not that.' She didn't want to tell him the real reason right now. It wasn't the time or the place, and she still didn't have the right words to explain the situation to him. 'So do you have an answer for Sara?'

'Yes. I agree with you, so I've marked on her notes that I'm happy for her to have an elective section. I'll get it booked in with Theatre. Do you want me to come and have a word with her?'

'No, it's fine.' Especially as that coffee was making her feel queasy again and she didn't want to have to dash off to the toilets again and risk him working out what was really going on. 'Thanks. I'd better get back to my patient. Catch you later.'

Ella was acting really oddly, Oliver thought. Rushing out of his office like that. Yet she'd been adamant that she wasn't going down with the sickness bug that was sweeping through the hospital.

So what was the problem?

Things had been awkward between them ever since the night of the masked ball. The night when he'd taken her virginity. He still felt guilty about it; and as a result he'd probably been even more cool with her than she was being with him.

He really ought to have a chat with her and

try to get things back on an even keel between them. Especially as he was the Assistant Head of Obstetrics now. There was absolutely no way they could get involved with each other; although he wasn't directly her boss, he was her senior. Though it would be nice to salvage some kind of working relationship, so they were at least on semi-friendly terms in the department. He *liked* Ella. He missed the easiness between them.

As for anything more… Well, he'd told her the truth. He wasn't a good bet when it came to relationships. Even though Ella was the one woman he thought might actually tempt him to try, it just couldn't happen. It would all go wrong and wreck their working relationship for good.

He knew she'd be writing up her notes after her appointments, so he quickly typed out a message on the hospital's internal email system.

We need to have a chat. Come and see me when you're done today.

Before he hit 'send', he added 'please', so she'd know he wasn't being cold and snooty with her. And hopefully they could sort things out.

We need to have a chat. Come and see me when you're done today, please.

Oh, help. That sounded very formal and very ominous, Ella thought as she read the email at the end of her shift. Why did Oliver want to see her?

She hadn't put a foot wrong in her job ever since she'd moved from London to Teddy's eighteen months ago. But, now Oliver was Assistant Head of Obstetrics, he was bound to have read everyone's file, to help him get a handle on the team and see where anyone might need more training. If he'd read her file, then he'd know that she'd only just scraped through her exams at university. Was this why he wanted to see her? Did this mean he was going to expect her to prove herself all over again?

Great. Just the thing to start off a Saturday evening. Not.

Dreading what he was going to say, she went to Oliver's office. 'You wanted to see me?'

He looked up from his desk. 'Yes. Close the door, please.'

Now that was *really* worrying. Was he about to tell her that he was reorganising the team and there wasn't a space for her? She couldn't think why else he would reverse his usual open-door policy.

Adrenalin slid down her spine, and she did as he'd asked.

'We need to talk,' he said, gesturing to the chair opposite his.

'Right.' She sat down.

'Coffee?'

Even the thought of it made her gag. She tried really hard to stop the reflex, using the trick her dentist had taught her last time she'd had to have an X-ray by making a fist of her left hand, squeezing her thumb with her fingers. Except it didn't help and she still found herself gagging.

'Are you all right, Ella?' Oliver asked.

'Mmm,' she fibbed. 'Maybe some water would help.'

He narrowed his eyes at her. 'What aren't you telling me?'

Oh, help. She wasn't ready for this conversation. At all. And it made it worse that every time she looked at him, she remembered what it felt like to be in his arms. What it felt like to kiss him. What it felt like when his bare skin was sliding against hers…

And this wasn't the time and the place for remembering that, either. 'Why did you want to see me?' she asked instead of answering his question. 'Am I losing my job?'

'Losing your job?' Oliver looked surprised. 'Of course not. Why would you think that?'

'Your note was pretty ominous.'

He frowned. 'It was meant to be polite.'

'And you just asked me to close the door…'

'I'm not sacking you, Ella, and this isn't a disciplinary meeting, if that's what you're thinking.' He raked a hand through his hair. 'Things are a bit strained between us and I wanted to clear the air, that's all. Look, let me grab you some water or some coffee, and we can—' He stopped abruptly. 'Ella, you've gone green. Are you quite sure you're not going down with the sickness bug?'

'I'm sure.'

'Then what's wrong?'

She couldn't see her way out of this. She was going to have to tell him at some point, so it might as well be now. And she'd had all afternoon to think about how to tell him and still hadn't come up with the right words. Maybe short and to the point would be the best option. 'I'm pregnant,' she said miserably.

Pregnant?

Oliver's head spun and he actually had to shake his head physically to clear it.

Pregnant.

He'd been here before. With Justine. Except the baby hadn't been his, because Justine had lied to him all along. He knew Ella was nothing like Justine; but the past still haunted him.

The last time those words had been said to him, he'd been just as shocked. The baby hadn't been planned and he'd still been studying for his specialist exams. He hadn't been ready for the extra responsibility of parenthood, but of course he'd done the right thing and stood by Justine. It was his duty.

And then, when Justine had finally told him the truth, he'd been let off the hook. Except by then he'd started to think of himself as a dad. Having that taken away from him had hurt even more than Justine's betrayal. He'd been shocked by how isolated and lost he'd felt—and he'd sworn that never again would he let himself get emotionally involved or in a position where someone could hurt him like that.

Now here he was again, hearing a woman tell him that she was expecting his baby. Even though Ella came from a completely different background, and he'd worked with her for long enough to trust her on a lot of levels—the situation brought back all the hurt and mistrust.

'How pregnant?' he asked carefully.

'My last period was the middle of October. I'm nearly three weeks late.'

'Seven weeks, then,' he said, calculating rapidly. They'd had unprotected sex on the night of the Hallowe'en ball. That would've been two weeks after the start of her last period, from what she'd just said. Which meant they'd had sex right in the middle of her cycle: the most fertile time.

And she'd been a virgin—something that made him feel guilty and protective of her at the same time. And which put all kind of inappropriate memories in his head: the way her voice had gone all husky with arousal, the way her pupils had gone wide and dark with desire, the way it had felt when he'd finally eased into her...

Oh, for pity's sake. He couldn't think of that now. She'd just told him she was pregnant.

Of course it was his baby. There was no question that it was anyone else's baby. Everyone knew that Ella was completely devoted to her job—come to think of it, she hadn't dated anyone since he'd known her.

Except for that one snatched evening with him. And he'd been the only man who'd ever shared her bed like that—with the ultimate closeness. Which made it special, because Ella wasn't the sort to sleep around.

She looked anxious. 'So you believe me?'

'That you're pregnant? Or that it's mine? Obviously the dates tally. And, given the situation, it's pretty obvious that the baby's mine.' He looked at her. 'I assume you've done a test, to be this sure about it?'

She nodded. 'Today.'

'And you didn't suspect anything before today?'

She frowned. 'No.'

'Even though your period was late?'

'I put that down to stress,' she said. 'You know it's been crazy round here, with so many people off sick, plus Sienna's going off on maternity leave really soon and it'll take Max a while to settle in properly. We're all rushed off our feet.'

'So what made you decide to do a test today?' Then he remembered how she'd run out of his office, admitting afterwards that she'd felt a bit sick. He'd assumed she was going down with the bug. But it hadn't been that at all. 'You started getting morning sickness,' he said, answering his own question.

She nodded. 'I can't bear the smell of strong aftershave and coffee. That's what made me...' She swallowed hard, obviously feeling queasy at just the thought of the scents.

He grabbed one of the bottles of water he kept in his desk drawer and pushed it across the desk at her. 'Here.'

'Thank you.' She unscrewed the cap and took a sip of water. 'Oliver, I didn't mean this to happen. I wasn't trying to trap you, or try to sleep my way up the ladder or anything like that. It wasn't planned.'

'Too right it wasn't planned,' he said grimly. He wasn't angry with her, but he was furious with himself. Why hadn't he taken proper responsibility when it came to precautions? More to the point, why had he made love with her in the first place, when he'd managed to keep his hands to himself and his libido under control for the last eighteen months? Why had he given into temptation that night, let the single glass of champagne he'd drunk go completely to his head and wipe out his inhibitions enough to let him kiss her and take her to bed?

Though he really wasn't prepared to answer those questions right now.

Instead, to cover up his guilt and confusion, he snapped at her. 'So what was it? The Pill didn't work?'

She flinched. 'I'm not on the Pill.'

What? He could hardly believe what he was hearing. 'You led me to believe you were.' So, in a way, she'd been as devious as Justine. Clearly his judgement was incredibly poor when it came to relationships.

'I didn't say I was on the Pill.'

'You hinted at it.' He remembered it very clearly. 'You said I didn't need a condom. Why would you say that unless you were taking the Pill?'

'Well, that lets you very nicely off the hook, doesn't it? Because it's all my fault. That's fine. I accept the entire blame for the situation.' She screwed the cap back on the water bottle. 'Don't worry, Mr Darrington, I'm not expecting any-thing from you. I just thought you had the right to know about the baby.' She stood up. 'I'm of-ficially off duty right now, so I'm going home.'

'Wait. Ella.' He blew out a breath. 'You've just told me you're expecting my baby. At least give me time to process the news. And what do you mean, you're not expecting anything from me? As the baby's father, of course I'll support you financially.' Just as he'd supported Justine when he'd thought that she was pregnant with his baby. A Darrington always did the right thing.

'I don't want your money.'

'Tough. Because I have no intention of letting you go through this unsupported and on your own.' He stared at her. One thing he was very sure about: this time he wasn't going to have fatherhood snatched away from him. This time he was exercising his rights, and he was going to have *choices*. 'It's my baby, too, Ella. So that means I get a say. In *everything*.'

'I never had you pegged as an overbearing bully,' she said, 'but you're behaving like one right now. I'm telling you about the baby purely out of courtesy, and I know you're not interested in being with me so I don't expect anything from you. And now, if you'll excuse me, I've already told you I'm off duty and I want to go home. Goodnight.'

This time, she walked out.

By the time Oliver had gathered his thoughts enough to think of going after her, Ella was nowhere to be seen.

Great.

If he ran after her now, everybody would notice. The last thing either of them needed right now was to have the hospital speculating about their relationship—or, worse still, actually guessing that Ella was pregnant with his baby.

He needed time to think about this. To get used

to the idea. To work out exactly what he was going to do.

So much for thinking that he and Ella could smooth over what had happened that night and try to repair their working relationship. Her bombshell had just changed everything. And right at that moment he didn't have a clue what to do next, or even what to think. She hadn't even told him why she hadn't been on the Pill, and he needed to get to the bottom of that. His head was spinning.

He'd finish all the admin here and then go for a run to clear his head. And then, maybe, he'd be able to work out the best way forward. For all three of them.

The run cleared his head a bit. But then the reality slammed home. He was going to be a father.

Oliver took a deep breath. He'd been here before, but this time he had no doubts at all. The baby was his, and so was the responsibility. OK, so she'd told him he didn't need to use protection, and that had turned out not to be true—but it took two to make a baby. Plus Ella's family lived hundreds of miles away in Ireland; although her best friend lived in Cheltenham, it basically meant that Ella was on her own. She and the baby needed him to step up to the plate and be responsible.

He could start by making sure that she was taking folic acid and eating properly. Which was hard in the early stages, when you had morning sickness and couldn't face the smell or taste of certain foods. He now knew the smell of coffee was a trigger for her, so he needed to find something that was bland, yet nutritious and tempting at the same time. Decaffeinated tea might be easier for her than coffee; he knew she usually drank tea at work. And maybe some fresh strawberries, pasteurised yoghurt and granola.

He dropped in to the supermarket on his way home, trying to ignore the piped Christmassy music and the stacks of Christmas chocolates and goodies displayed throughout the shop. Right now it didn't feel much like Christmas. It felt as if the world had been shaken upside down and he wasn't quite sure what day it was. Though he rather thought he might need some kind of Christmas miracle right now.

He concentrated on picking out things he

thought might tempt Ella to eat, and added a box of vitamins specially formulated for pregnant women. Then he came to the large stand of flowers by the tills. Did Ella even like flowers? He didn't have a clue. He knew some women hated cut flowers, preferring to let them bloom in a garden or on an indoor plant. And there was the scent issue. Something as strong as lilies might set off her morning sickness.

But it would be a gesture. A start. A way of showing her that he wanted to be on the same side. Maybe something not over-the-top and showy, like the large bouquets sprinkled with artificial snow and glitter. Something a little smaller and bright and cheerful with no scent, like the bunch of sunny yellow gerbera. Although he didn't have a vase at home, he could stick them in a large glass of water overnight so they'd still look nice in the morning. Hopefully Ella would like them.

Then maybe tomorrow they could talk sensibly about their options. Hopefully Ella would tell him what she really wanted. She'd said that she was only telling him about the baby out of courtesy, but did she really mean that? Did she want him to be part of the baby's life—part of *her* life? Or did she really mean to do what their colleague Sienna seemed to be doing, and go it alone?

And what did he want?

Since Justine's betrayal, Oliver had major trust issues when it came to relationships. He didn't date seriously. He hadn't even wanted a proper relationship, thinking that the risks of getting hurt again were too high. But the fact that Ella was expecting his baby changed that. He knew he definitely wanted to be a part of his child's life.

And Ella? He'd fought against his attraction towards her for months, keeping it strictly professional between them at work. Then, the night of the charity ball, he'd danced with her; it had felt so right to hold her in his arms. To kiss her, when he'd driven her home. To make love with her, losing himself inside her.

If he was honest with himself, he wanted to do it again. And more. He wanted to wake up with her curled in his arms. Being with Ella had made him feel that the world was full of sunshine. That snatched evening was the first time he'd felt really connected with anyone for years. He could actually see them as a family: Ella nursing the baby at the kitchen table, chatting to him about his day when he got home from work. Going to the park, with himself pushing the pram and Ella by his side—maybe with a little dog, too. Reading a bedtime story to the baby together and doing all the voices between them.

They could give their baby the kind of childhood he hadn't had. One filled with warmth and love.

But then reality slammed in. Did she feel the same way about him? Did she want to make a family with him, or did she just want financial support, the way Justine had? OK, so she didn't know who his parents were, and she'd said earlier that she didn't want his money—but was it true?

Had it meant anything to her, giving him her virginity? Or had it all just been a nuisance to her, an embarrassment, something she wanted to get rid of and he'd happened to be in a convenient place to do her a favour? And why had she been so adamant that they didn't need contraception—especially as it now turned out that she hadn't been on the Pill?

He didn't have a clue. In normal circumstances,

that would be a difficult conversation to have. With pregnancy hormones clouding the issue, it was going to be even harder.

Tomorrow.

He'd sleep on it and hope that the right words would lodge themselves in his head by tomorrow.

CHAPTER TWO

ON SUNDAY MORNING, Oliver drove over to the pretty little square where Ella's flat was and rang her doorbell.

She opened the door wearing pyjamas, sleepy-eyed and with her hair all mussed. 'I'm sorry. I didn't mean to wake you,' he said.

'It's almost half-past nine, so it's my bad,' she said wryly. 'What do you want?'

He held up the recyclable shopping bag. 'I brought breakfast. I thought maybe we could talk.'

'Breakfast?'

'And these.' He handed her the gerbera. 'I hope you like them.'

Unexpectedly, her beautiful green eyes filled with tears. 'Oliver, they're gorgeous. I love yellow flowers. Thank you. Though you really didn't have to do that.'

'I wanted to,' he admitted. And right now, seeing her all warm and sleepy, he really wanted to take her in his arms and hold her close and tell her that he'd protect her from the world.

Except he wasn't sure how she'd react, and he knew he needed to take this slowly and carefully until he had a better idea of what was going on in her head. He wasn't going to end up in the same place he'd been after Justine, where he'd been in love with her but she hadn't loved him back.

'Come in. I'll put the kettle on.' She ushered him through to her living room. 'I'll go and have a quick shower and get dressed, and then I'll put those lovely flowers in water.'

'You don't have to change on my behalf.'

She gave him a speaking glance. 'I can't be sitting here at my kitchen table in pyjamas, with you all dressed up like a magazine model.'

'Apart from the fact that I'm not all dressed up, I don't mind if you stay in your pyjamas.'

'Well, *I* do.'

He really didn't want to sit around doing nothing. It wasn't his style. He'd always preferred keeping busy. 'Shall I make breakfast, then, while you're showering?'

He could see that she was torn between insisting that it was her flat so it was her job to make breakfast, and letting him do something. 'All right,' she said finally. 'I normally eat in the kitchen, if that's all right with you.'

'OK. I'll see you when you're ready.'

By the time Ella had showered and changed into jeans and a cute Christmassy sweater with a reindeer in a bow tie on the front, Oliver had laid two places at the tiny bistro table in her kitchen and had arranged everything on the table: freshly squeezed orange juice, granola, yoghurt and a bowl of hulled and washed strawberries. It looked amazing. And she couldn't remember the last time anyone apart from her parents had made this kind of fuss over her. Right now she felt cherished—special—and it was a good feeling.

'No coffee,' he said.

'Thanks. I really can't bear the smell of it.'

'And that's why I held off on the croissants. Just in case they affected you, too.' He gestured to the teapot. 'The tea's decaf—I thought it might be easier for you to manage.'

'That's so sweet.' He'd made all this effort just

for her, and her heart melted. 'This all looks so nice. Thank you.'

'I had to guess because I didn't really know what kind of thing you like for breakfast.'

She blushed. 'You didn't stay for breakfast when... Well, you know.'

'Uh-huh.'

Right at that moment, he looked just as embarrassed and awkward as she felt. She'd been stupid to bring up the issue.

'I just wanted to do something nice for you,' he said.

'And I appreciate it,' she said meaning it.

He poured her a mug of tea. 'No sugar, right?'

She loved the fact that he'd actually noticed how she took her tea. 'Right.'

'So how are you feeling?' he asked.

'Mostly fine. Just as long as I avoid strong smells.' She smiled. 'And that should get better in about six weeks, or so I always tell my mums.'

'It's usually better by the second trimester,' he agreed.

'I thought Sienna was teasing me when she told me that tin cans actually smell when you're pregnant,' Ella said, 'but she's right. They do.'

She shuddered, and took a sip of the orange juice. 'This is lovely. Thank you so much. I feel totally spoiled.'

'It's the least I could do.' Again, Oliver could imagine having breakfast with Ella on Sunday mornings. A lazy breakfast, with toast and tea and the Sunday papers, and then taking the baby out together for a late-morning walk in the park... It shocked him to discover how much he actually wanted that.

A real relationship.

With Ella and their baby.

Thankfully she hadn't noticed him mooning about, because she asked, 'So is everything OK with you?'

'Yes.'

'And you're settling in well to your new job?'

'Just about,' he said, smiling back at her. Maybe this was going to work out. They could at least make polite conversation. And they'd been friends before the masked ball. They respected each other as colleagues. He really believed they could salvage something from this now.

He kept the conversation going until they'd finished breakfast and he started clearing the table; then he noticed that there was still something left in the bag he'd brought with him. 'Oh, I meant to give you this earlier.' He took the box of vitamins from the bag and handed them to her.

She frowned. 'What's this?'

'Folic acid—obviously now you know about the baby, you need to start taking it.'

'Uh-huh.' Her face shuttered. 'Did it occur to you that I might already have bought a pregnancy vitamin supplement with folic acid?'

'I—' He stared at her. No. He hadn't given it a second thought.

'Oliver, I'm a midwife. It'd be a bit stupid of me to ignore my years of training about the best way for pregnant women to look after themselves and their babies, wouldn't it?'

She sounded really put out, though he couldn't for the life of him understand why. All he'd done was buy her some vitamins. 'I was just trying to help. To look after you.'

'To take over, more like,' she said.

'But—'

'Do you think I'm suffering from "pregnancy brain" and I'm completely flaky?' she asked. She shook her head, narrowing her eyes at him. 'And, for your information, "pregnancy brain" is a total myth. I came across a piece on the news the other day that said actually women's brains are sharper when they're pregnant.'

What? Where was all this coming from? He didn't understand. 'Ella, I didn't accuse you of anything of the sort.'

'No, but you bought me folic acid without even thinking that I might already have some. There's a huge difference between asking me if you can pick something up for me, and just presenting me with it as if I'm too stupid to have thought of it for myself.'

'You're overreacting.'

'Am I?' She folded her arms. 'If this is how it's going to be for the next seven and a half months, with you looking over my shoulder all the time and making decisions for me without even bothering to discuss things with me first...' Again, she shook her head. 'That's really overbearing and that's not what I want, Oliver. Actually, right now I think I'd like you to leave and give me some space.'

He stared at her in disbelief. 'All I want to do

is to protect you and the baby, and provide for you. How's that being overbearing?'

Could he really not see it? Ella wondered. 'It's overbearing because you're not discussing any-thing with me. You've made the decision already and you're expecting me to just shut up and go along with it.' She'd been there before: when everyone thought that little Ella wasn't bright enough to train as a midwife. She hated the way Oliver seemed to be falling into those same at-titudes and thinking he knew what was best for her. She'd had years of feeling undermined and useless, and she wasn't going to let it happen again. 'And if you *dare* say that's just pregnancy hormones making me grumpy, I'll…I'll…' She was too angry to think of what she'd do next. So much for thinking he wanted to cherish her. What an idiot she was, letting herself fall a little more in love with a control freak who wanted to boss her around.

'Ella, this is—'

'I need some space. Thank you for the flow-ers and breakfast, because that was very nice of you, but I'd really like you to leave now. Please.'

'What about the washing up?'

'I think I might just about be capable of sorting that out for myself.' She stood up and gestured to the doorway. 'Would you give me some space, please?'

Maybe making a tactical retreat would be the best thing to do right now, Oliver thought. 'All right.'

He wasn't sure whether her reaction had made him more hurt or angry. He'd tried to do the right thing, but Ella was being totally unreasonable. He'd never called her intelligence into question. Why on earth would she think he had?

Despite her protests, he was pretty sure that pregnancy hormones were affecting her mood.

He'd try to talk to her again later and hope that she'd be in a better frame of mind. More receptive.

Going to the gym and pounding the treadmill didn't help. Neither did going to his office and spending a couple of hours catching up on paperwork.

Was he really being overbearing and making decisions without asking her? Oliver wondered.

A simple box of vitamins really shouldn't cause this much trouble.

Justine had been more than happy for him to make a fuss of her and buy things for her while she was pregnant. Then again, she'd had her reasons. But Ella was seriously independent. Brave enough to travel to London at the age of eighteen to study midwifery, so far from her family home in Ireland that she wouldn't be able to just pop home for the weekend like most of the other students could. And she'd be brave enough to bring up this baby on her own.

Except she didn't have to.

He wanted to be there. For her and for the baby.

He didn't want to tell her about Justine—not just yet—but he could try to build a bridge. Try to see things from Ella's point of view.

It didn't take him long to drive back to her flat.

This time, when she answered the doorbell, she didn't smile.

'Hear me out?' he asked. 'Please?'

She said nothing, but at least she didn't slam the door in his face. 'I was going to get you flowers as an apology, but I already bought you flowers this morning and I don't want you to think I'm going over the top—especially as you already think I'm being overbearing. I had no idea what to get you. I don't know what you like, so I just...' Oliver hated feeling so clueless and awkward. Normally he was in charge and he knew everything would go smoothly. This was way out of his comfort zone.

'It doesn't matter. I don't need you to buy me things.'

Another difference between Ella and the women he usually dated: they expected presents. Expensive presents.

'The most important thing is that I'm sorry for being bossy. I don't mean to be and I'll try not to be. But,' he said, 'old habits die hard, and I can't promise that I won't mess up in the future.'

Her face softened, then, as if she understood the jumble of thoughts filling his head, and she stepped back from the doorway. 'Come in and I'll make some tea—and, for the record, I'm perfectly capable of filling a kettle with water and boiling it.'

'I know,' he said. He'd got the message that Ella liked her independence. 'But is there anything I can do to help?'

'Just sit down and let me do it myself.'

He waited on the sofa in the living room, feeling more and more antsy as the seconds passed.

Finally, she came in with two mugs of tea.

'Thank you,' he said, accepting one of the mugs.

She inclined her head in acknowledgement and sat down at her desk rather than next to him on the sofa. Making a point, he supposed.

'It must be difficult for you, being in this situation,' she said.

That was an understatement. She didn't know anything about the memories it was bringing back, and right at the moment it wasn't something he wanted to share. 'It's not exactly a picnic for you, either,' he said, trying to see it from her point of view. 'All I need to do is to get my head round this properly.' *All.* He was struggling enough with that. 'But it's worse for you because you get all the morning sickness and what have you as well.'

'Thanks for reminding me,' she said dryly.

'Ella, I want to be there for you and the baby.'

'I understand that. But it doesn't give you the right to push me around.'

He hadn't been trying to push her around, but he didn't want to argue. Now was probably not the right time to ask difficult questions about the contraception issue, either. He wanted to get their relationship on a less rocky footing, first. Instead, he asked carefully, 'So have you thought about what kind of care you want, and whether you want to book in at Teddy's or if you'd rather go somewhere else?'

'I know all the staff at Teddy's and I know I'll get the best care there, so it makes sense to book in to our department,' she said. 'Though it does mean everyone's going to know. And at a really early stage.'

'Is that a problem?'

She looked thoughtful. 'I guess not—I mean, everyone's been great about Sienna. After the initial gossip, wondering who the baby's father is.'

'Would you prefer people not to know I'm the baby's father?'

'I don't want people thinking I slept with you to get an advantage at work.'

He smiled. 'Ella, nobody would ever think that of you. You work hard enough for two people as it is.' He paused. 'What about a scan?'

'I already know I'm about seven weeks.'

'Which is about the right time for a dating scan—not that I disbelieve you on the dates, just...'

She nodded. 'Though it'll mean people will know now, not later on.'

'Yes, and they'll cut you a bit of slack—this is the stage where you're likely to feel really tired and need a break.'

'I'll still be part of the team, and being pregnant doesn't alter that.'

Why was she being so difficult about this? 'I'm not saying that you're not part of the team—just that maybe you could cut back a bit on your shifts for a while.'

Her face darkened. 'No.'

'Ella—'

'I said before, please don't push me around. You're not my keeper, Oliver.'

'I know. I'm just trying to do what's best for you.'

'Because I'm not bright enough to know what's best for me?'

'No, of course not.' He didn't get why she was

being so prickly. 'Ella, is there something you're not telling me?'

'How do you mean?'

'You and me—we've always got on well. Until—well.' He didn't want to embarrass her by putting it into words.

But she clearly wanted to face it head-on. 'Until we slept together.'

'I feel guilty about that. You're not the sort who does one-night stands—and I took your virginity.'

'Which isn't an issue.'

'It is for me.'

She looked confused. 'Why?'

'Because it makes me feel dishonourable.'

She scoffed. 'Oh, get over yourself, Oliver. What are you, the Lord of the Manor?'

Not far off it. But he needed to get back on reasonable terms with her before he dropped that particular bombshell. 'I'm sorry. I did warn you I'd mess up on the control freakery stuff.'

'I guess. And maybe I need to cut you some slack, too—but how would you feel if I suggested you cut back on your shifts, just because you'll have a baby in seven months' time?'

He nodded. 'I get it.'

She rubbed her stomach reflectively. 'So is there a new girlfriend who might not be very happy to hear the news?'

'No, there isn't.' And the question stung. 'Do you really think I'm that shallow?'

'No, but you never seem to date anyone for long.'

'Strictly speaking, I didn't actually date you,' he pointed out. 'We both got carried away, that night.'

'I guess.' She paused. 'So why do you avoid proper relationships?'

Something else he didn't want to discuss. 'Let's just say I've been a bit burned in the past.'

'And you're still brooding over it enough not to give someone else a chance? She must've hurt you a lot.'

'Yes. She did,' he admitted.

'I'm sorry that you got hurt. But I'm nothing like the usual women you date.'

'Usual?'

She grimaced. 'I haven't been gossiping about you. But the hospital grapevine says you pick women who look like models, women from a much posher background than mine.'

He stared at her. 'You think I'm a snob?'

'No. You treat all our mums the same, whether they're ordinary women or royalty or celebs,' she said. 'I guess what I'm saying is I'm me, so don't go thinking I'll be like her.'

'You're not like her.' He trusted Ella, for a start. Professionally. But letting her into his heart would take a lot longer. Justine had left him with a lot of baggage.

Though he really didn't want to talk to Ella about Justine right now. Especially given their circumstances. How did you tell someone who was expecting your baby that you'd been here before—but the baby hadn't been yours? She'd start reading all kinds of things into that and what he might be thinking now, and he was having a hard time explaining it to himself; he certainly couldn't explain his feelings to her. Wanting to change the subject, he asked, 'What about you?'

Her eyes widened. 'You seriously think I'd date someone else when I'm pregnant with your baby?'

He winced. 'That sounds bad. I mean… You

only just found out about the baby. You might've met someone between Hallowe'en and now.'

'No. There isn't anyone.'

'OK.'

And actually the hospital grapevine said she didn't date. Ella was dedicated to her work. Oliver assumed that someone had hurt her badly in the past and she didn't trust love any more, the same way that he didn't trust love. But he could hardly grill her about it. That would be intrusive; besides, right now their relationship was so fragile he didn't want to risk saying the wrong thing and making it worse. 'Have you told your parents?' he asked.

'Not yet. I think I'd prefer to do that face to face—video-calling isn't good enough for news like this,' she said. 'I'm going home for two days at Christmas. I'll tell them then.'

'How do you think they'll take it?'

With sheer disbelief, Ella thought. Her parents knew the situation with her endometriosis and the ruptured cyst. They'd resigned themselves to never having grandchildren, though she'd seen the wistfulness in her mum's eyes every time one of her sisters became a grandmother again. Not that she wanted to discuss any of that with Oliver. Not right now. Because if he knew about her medical issues from the past, he'd try even harder to wrap her in cotton wool and it would drive her crazy.

'They'll be supportive,' she said. She knew that without having to ask. They might be shocked, but they'd definitely be supportive. 'How about yours?'

'It's complicated,' he said.

Another stonewall. Oliver had been hurt by someone in the past and his family situation was complicated. Did that mean maybe his ex had dumped him for his brother, or something? Did he even have a brother or a sister? But, even if she asked him straight out, she knew he'd evade the subject. 'You don't give anything away, do you?'

'I…' He blew out a breath. 'I'm making a mess of this.'

'Yes, you are,' she said. 'It's always better to be honest.' Which was pretty hypocritical of her, considering what she was keeping from him.

He raked a hand through his hair. 'Ella, right now all that matters to me is you and the baby.'

Why couldn't she let herself believe him?

When she didn't say anything, he sighed. 'I'd really like to be there at the scan. But it's your call.'

That was quite a capitulation—and one that clearly hadn't come easily to him. He was used to being in charge at work, so of course he was going to be bossy outside work as well. And maybe she had overreacted a bit. Maybe he really *had* meant to be helpful and trying to look after her, rather than making her feel stupid. But she didn't want to whine about her dyslexia. Plenty of people had more to deal with than she did.

Maybe she should capitulate a bit, too. 'I'll let you know when I've seen my doctor and got a date through,' she said.

'Thank you.' He finished his tea. 'I guess I should let you have the rest of your afternoon in peace. But call me if you need anything, OK? And I'm not trying to be bossy. I'm trying to be supportive.'

'Uh-huh.'

When she'd shown him out, she tidied up and

washed up the mugs. She had absolutely no idea how this was going to work out. Oliver was clearly intending to do the right thing and stand by her—but she didn't want him to be with her out of duty. She wanted him there because he *wanted* to be there.

He hadn't said a word about his feelings. He hadn't asked her about hers, either. Which was just as well, because she was all mixed up. The attraction she'd felt towards him hadn't gone away, but she was pretty sure it was one-sided. She didn't want him to pity her for mooning about over him, so she'd been sharper towards him than normal. But then again, if it was that easy to push him away, he clearly didn't want to be with her in the first place.

'It'll work out,' she said quietly, cradling her abdomen protectively with one hand. 'If the worst comes to the worst, I'll go back home to my family in Ireland. But one thing I promise you, baby: even though you weren't planned, you'll always, *always* be loved. And if you're a girl I'm going to call you Joy, because that's what you are to me.'

CHAPTER THREE

ELLA WAS ON a late shift on the Monday morning, and called her GP's surgery as soon as they were open. To her surprise and delight, the GP was able to see her that morning before her shift.

'How are you feeling?' the GP asked when Ella told her she was pregnant.

'Fairly shocked,' Ella admitted. 'I didn't think this would ever happen, after what the doctors told me in London. But, now I've had a couple of days to get used to the idea, I'm thrilled.'

'Good.' The GP smiled. 'Congratulations. Are you having any symptoms?'

'A bit of morning sickness—it's not much fun if one of the dads-to-be on the ward is wearing a ton of aftershave, or if anyone at work's drinking coffee,' Ella admitted.

'I don't need to tell you that you should feel a lot better by the time you're twelve weeks.'

Ella smiled back. 'No. It's weird, because I'm usually the one giving that advice.'

'And you've already done a test?' the GP asked.

'Yes.'

'Then there's not much point in doing a second one,' the GP said. 'Given your medical history, though, I'd like to send you for an early scan. As you work at Teddy's, would you rather go there or would you prefer to book in for your antenatal care somewhere else?'

'Teddy's is fine,' Ella confirmed.

'Good. I'll put a call through to the ultrasound department this morning. Reception will contact you with the date and time.'

'That's great—thank you very much.'

By the time Ella got to Teddy's, the GP's surgery had already sent her a text with the date and time of her scan. Ella wasn't sure whether she was more relieved or shocked to discover that the scan was tomorrow morning, an hour before her shift was due to start.

Someone was bound to see her in the waiting room for the ultrasound, so the whole department would know about the baby very quickly. Which meant that Ella needed to find Annabelle and tell her the news herself. The last thing she wanted was for her best friend to hear about the baby from hospital gossip, especially as she knew what Annabelle had been through over the last few years.

Annabelle was in her office, clearly writing up some reports. Ella knocked on the door, opened it slightly and leaned through the gap. 'I can see you're really busy,' she said, 'but can I have a quick word?'

'Sure,' Annabelle said. 'Is everything all right?'

'Yes—there's just something I wanted to tell you.' Then Ella looked more closely at her friend. 'There's something different about you.'

'How do you mean, different?' Annabelle asked.

'You look happier than I've seen you in a long, long time.'

Annabelle smiled. 'That's because Max and I are back together. For good.'

'Really?' Thrilled for her friend, Ella leaned over the desk and hugged her. 'That's fabulous news.'

'All those years I thought I'd failed him because I couldn't give him children.' Annabelle blew out a breath. 'But he says I'm enough for him, Ella. He doesn't need a family to feel we're complete.'

'I'm so pleased.' Ella paused. 'So this means you're not going to try IVF again?'

'No. We might consider adopting in the future, but we need time to think about it. And time just to enjoy each other,' Annabelle said. 'So what's your news?'

Even though Annabelle seemed to be OK with the idea of not trying for a family, Ella knew that this was still a sensitive subject. 'There isn't an easy way to say this.'

'Oh, no. Please don't tell me you're leaving Teddy's.'

'No.' At least, she hoped she wasn't going to have to leave. 'Annabelle, I wanted you to know before anyone else on the ward does—because everyone's going to know after tomorrow. And I really don't want this to upset you.'

'Now you're really worrying me. Is it another cyst?' Annabelle bit her lip. 'Or—and I *really* hope it isn't—something more sinister?'

Ella took a deep breath. 'No. Nothing like that.'

'Then will you please put me out of my misery?'

'I'm pregnant.'

'Pregnant?' Annabelle's blue eyes widened. 'That's the last thing I expected *you* to tell me. But—how?'

Ella squirmed. 'Basic biology?'

'Apart from the fact that you're not dating anyone—or, if you are, you haven't told me about him—there's your endometriosis and that ruptured cyst and all the damage to your Fallopian tubes,' Annabelle pointed out. 'I thought the doctors in London said there was no chance of you conceiving?'

'They did. But I guess there was a billion to one chance after all.' A Christmas miracle. One Ella had never dared to dream about.

'I don't know what to say. Are you…well, happy about it?' Annabelle asked cautiously.

Ella nodded. Yet, at the same time, part of her was sad. This wasn't how she'd dreamed of things being when she was a child; she'd imagined having a partner who loved her. That definitely wasn't the situation with Oliver.

'Congratulations. I'm so pleased for you.' Annabelle hugged her. 'How far are you?'

'Seven weeks.'

'Your mum will be over the moon at the idea of being a granny.'

Ella smiled. 'I know. I'm going to tell her at Christmas when I go back to Ireland. Or maybe I'll take a snap of the scan photograph on my phone and send it to her tomorrow.'

'You've got a dating scan tomorrow? That's fantastic. Do you want me to come with you?' Annabelle asked.

'That's lovely of you to offer, but it's fine.'

'Of course. I guess the dad will want to be there.'

Dear Annabelle. She was clearly dying to know who it was, but she wasn't going to push her friend to share all the details until Ella was ready.

'The dad,' Ella said, 'is being just a little bit bossy at the moment and trying to wrap me up in cotton wool.'

Annabelle raised an eyebrow. 'He doesn't know you very well, then?'

'It's complicated.' Ella took a deep breath. 'I'm not actually dating him. And I'm not sure I'm ready for everyone to know who it is.'

'Sienna, mark two?' Annabelle asked wryly.

'Well, that's your right if you want to keep it to yourself. And you know I have your back.'

Ella smiled. 'I know.' Which was precisely why she was going to tell her best friend the truth. 'Obviously this is totally confidential—it's Oliver.'

'Oliver?' Annabelle asked in a scandalised whisper. 'As in our Assistant Head of Obstetrics?'

Ella winced. Was it so unlikely? 'Yes.'

'But… When?'

'The night of the charity ball. We danced together. A lot. He drove me home. And we…' She shrugged. 'Well…'

'I had no idea you even liked him.'

'I've liked him since the moment I met him,' Ella admitted. 'But I never said anything because I always thought he was way out of my league.'

Annabelle scoffed. 'You're lovely, and anyone who says otherwise has me to answer to.'

'But you know what the hospital gossip's like. They say he only dates people a couple of times—and they're usually tall, willowy women who look like models or movie stars. As in the opposite of me.'

'You're beautiful,' Annabelle said loyally.

'Thank you, but we both know I'm not Oliver's type. I'm too short and too round. And he… Well.' Ella had absolutely no idea how Oliver felt about her. He was being overprotective, but was that because of the baby?

'So what are you going to do?' Annabelle asked.

'I'm still working that out,' Ella admitted.

'Is he going to support you?'

'He's pretty much driven me crazy—presenting me with a box of folic acid, telling me to cut back on my shifts…'

'Ah. The protective male instinct coming out. And you sent him away with a flea in his ear?'

Ella nodded. 'You know how hard I worked to get through my exams. I'm not going to give all that up now.'

'So what do you want him to do?'

'Be part of the baby's life,' Ella said promptly. 'And not boss me about. Except I want him to be there because he wants to be there, not just because he thinks he ought to be there.'

'What does he say?' Annabelle asked.

'It's—' But Ella didn't get the chance to finish

the conversation, because one of their colleagues came in, needing Annabelle to come and see a patient.

'We'll talk later,' Annabelle promised, on her way out of the door. Except Ella had a busy shift, starting with a normal delivery and then one that turned complicated, so she didn't have time to catch up with Annabelle.

Everything was fine in her second delivery; there were no signs of complications and no signs of distress as she monitored the baby.

But, as the mum started to push, Ella realised that she was having difficulty delivering the baby's face and head. The classic sign of the baby having a 'turtle neck' told her exactly what the problem was: shoulder dystocia, meaning that the baby's shoulder was stuck behind the mum's pubic bone. And in the meantime it meant that the umbilical cord was squashed, so the baby had less oxygenated blood reaching her.

'Sophie, I need you to stop pushing,' Ella said calmly. She turned to the trainee midwife who was working with her. 'Jennie, please can you go and find Charlie? Tell him we have a baby with shoulder dystocia, then get hold of whichever anaesthetist and neonatal specialist is on call and ask them to come here.'

'What's happening?' Sophie asked, looking anxious.

'Usually, after the baby's head is born, the head and body turns sideways so the baby's shoulders pass comfortably through your pelvis. But sometimes that doesn't happen because the baby's shoulder gets stuck behind your pubic bone,' Ella explained. 'That's what's happened here. So we need a bit of extra help to get the baby out safely, and that's why I've asked our obstetrician to come in. There will be a few people coming into the room and it'll seem crowded and a bit scary, but please try not to worry. We're just being super-cautious and making sure that someone's there immediately if we need them, though with any luck we won't need any of them.'

'Does this happen very often?' Sophie asked, clearly in distress.

'Maybe one in a hundred and fifty to one in two hundred births,' Ella said. 'Try not to worry, Sophie. I've seen this happen a few times before, and we can still deliver the baby normally—but right now I'm going to have to ask you to stop pushing and change your position a bit so we can get the baby's shoulder unstuck and deliver her safely.'

'Anything you say,' Sophie said. 'I just want my baby here safely.' A tear trickled down her face.

'I know.' Ella squeezed her hand. 'I promise you, it's all going to be fine. Now, I want you to lie on your back, then wriggle down so your bum's right at the very edge of the bed. Can you do that for me?'

'I think so.' Sophie panted a bit, clearly trying to hold back on pushing, and then moved down the bed according to Ella's directions.

Charlie came in with Jennie, followed by the anaesthetist and neonatal specialist. Ella introduced everyone to Sophie. 'Charlie, I want to try the McRoberts manoeuvre first,' she said quietly. It was the most effective method of getting a baby's shoulder unstuck, and would hopefully avoid Sophie having to have an emergency section.

'That's a sound decision,' Charlie said as he quickly assessed the situation. 'I've got another delivery, so if you're confident with this I'll leave you and the team. I'll be in the birthing suite next door—my patient's waters have just broken.

'I'm good, Charlie,' Ella said, then turned her attention back to Sophie as Charlie departed, leaving her to manage the birth.

'Sophie, I'd like you to bend your knees and pull your legs back towards your tummy,' Ella said. 'Jennie's here to help you. What that does is to change the angle of your spine and your pelvis and that gives the baby a little bit more room, and then hopefully we'll be able to get her shoulder out a lot more easily. You'll feel me pushing on your tummy—it shouldn't hurt, just feel like pressure, so tell me straight away if it starts to hurt, OK?'

'All right,' Sophie said.

While Jennie helped move Sophie's legs into position, Ella pressed on Sophie's abdomen just above her pubic bone. It wasn't quite enough to release the baby's stuck shoulder, and she sighed inwardly. 'Sophie, I'm afraid her shoulder's still stuck. I'm going to need to give you an episiotomy to help me get the baby out.'

'I don't care,' Sophie said, 'as long as my baby's all right.'

Which was what Ella was worried about. There was a risk of Sophie tearing and having a postpartum haemorrhage—but more worrying still was that the brachial plexus, a bundle of nerves in the baby's shoulder and arm, could be stretched too much during the birth and be damaged.

'OK. You'll feel a sharp scratch as I give you some local anaesthetic,' Ella said as she worked. 'And you won't feel the episiotomy at all.' Swiftly, she made the incision and then finally managed to deliver the baby's head.

'Here we go—I think someone's all ready to meet her mum.' She clamped the cord, cut it, and handed the baby to Sophie while mentally assessing the baby's Apgar score.

'Oh, she's so beautiful—my baby,' Sophie said.

The baby yelled, and everyone in the room smiled. 'That's what we like to hear,' Ella said softly. 'Welcome to the world, baby.'

While Ella stitched up the episiotomy, the neonatal specialist checked the baby over. 'I'm pleased to say you have a very healthy little girl,' she said. 'She's absolutely fine.'

Ella helped Sophie get the baby latched on, and the baby took a couple of sucks before falling fast asleep.

'We'll get you settled back on the ward, Sophie,' Ella said. 'But if you're worried about any-thing at all, at any time, you just call one of us.'

'I will. And thank you,' Sophie said, tears running down her face. 'I'm so glad she's here.'

Oliver called in to one of the side rooms to see Hestia Blythe; he'd delivered her baby the previous evening by Caesarean section, after a long labour that had failed to progress and then the baby had started showing signs of distress.

'How are you both doing?' he asked with a smile.

'Fine, thanks.' Hestia smiled back at him. 'I'm a little bit sore, and I'm afraid I made a bit of a fuss earlier.' She grimaced. 'I feel so stupid, especially because I know how busy the midwives are and I should've just shut up and let them get on with helping people who really need it.'

'You're a new mum who needed a bit of help—you're allowed to make a fuss until you get used to doing things,' Oliver said. 'Nobody minds.'

She gave him a rueful look. 'I needed help to get my knickers on this morning after my shower and it was so, so pathetic. I actually cried my eyes out about it. I mean—how feeble is that?'

'You're not the first and you definitely won't be the last. Remember, you had twenty-four hours of labour and then an emergency section,' Oliver said. 'I'd be very surprised if you didn't need help with things for a day or two. And the tears are perfectly normal with all the hormones rushing round your body.'

'That's what that lovely midwife said—Ella— she was so kind,' Hestia told him. 'She said it was the baby blues kicking in early and everything will seem much better in a couple of days.'

'She's right. When you've had a bit of sleep and a chance to get over the operation, you'll feel a lot more settled,' Oliver agreed. And, yes, Ella was lovely with the patients. He'd noticed that even the most panicky new mums seemed to calm down around her.

'May I have a look at your scar, to see how you're healing?' he asked.

Hestia nodded. 'You kind of lose all your ideas of dignity when you have a baby, don't you?'

He smiled. 'We do try not to make you feel awkward about things, so please tell me if anything I say or do makes you uncomfortable. We want to make your stay here at Teddy's as good as it can be.'

'I didn't mean that,' she said, 'more that you don't feel shy or embarrassed about things any more—you get used to people looking at all the bits of you that aren't normally on view!'

'There is that,' Oliver agreed. He examined her scar. 'I'm pleased to say it looks as if you're healing very nicely. How's the baby?'

'He's feeding really well,' Hestia said. 'I found it a bit tricky to manage at first, but Ella sat down with me and showed me how to get the baby to latch on. She was really patient with me.'

'That's great. May I?' He indicated the crib next to the bed.

'Of course.'

Obviously she saw the goofy smile on his face when he looked at the baby because she said, 'You can pick him up and have a cuddle, if you like.'

'Yes, please.' Oliver grinned. 'This is one of my favourite parts of the job, cuddling a little one I helped to bring into the world. Hello, little man. How are you doing?' He lifted the baby tenderly and stroked the baby's cheek.

The baby yawned and opened his gorgeous dark blue eyes.

It was always a moment Oliver loved, when a newborn returned his gaze. But today it felt particularly special—because in a few months he knew he'd be doing this with his own baby. 'He's gorgeous, Hestia.'

'You're a natural at holding them,' Hestia said. 'Is that from your job, or do you have babies of your own?'

'My job,' he said. Though now he was going to have a baby of his own. And, the more he thought about the idea, the more it brought a smile to his face.

A baby.

His and Ella's.

Right now they weren't quite seeing eye to eye, but he'd make more of an effort. Because this really could work. He liked Ella and he knew she liked him. They were attracted to each other, or Hallowe'en wouldn't have happened. And love...? Oliver had stopped believing in that a long time ago. But he thought they could make a good life together, for the baby's sake.

He just needed to convince Ella.

'I was wondering,' Hestia said. 'My husband and I were talking, this morning, and you were so good with us last night. If it wasn't for you, we might not have our little boy now. And we'd like to name the baby after you. If that's all right?' she added.

'I'd be honoured,' Oliver said. 'Though I wasn't the only one in Theatre with you, so it'd be a bit greedy of me to take all the glory.'

'You were the one who saved our baby,' Hestia insisted. She peered over at his name tag. 'Oliver. That's such a lovely name.'

Oliver stared down at the baby. If Ella had a boy, would she want to call him Oliver? Or maybe Oliver as a middle name?

The baby started to grizzle and turn his head to the side. 'It looks as if someone's hungry.' He handed little Oliver over to his mum. 'Are you OK latching on now, or would you like me to get one of the midwives?'

'I'll manage—you've all been so great,' Hestia said.

'Good. If you need anything, let us know OK?'

'I will,' she promised. 'But right now all I can

think about is my little Oliver here. And how he's the best Christmas present I could've asked for.'

Oliver smiled at her and left the room.

The best Christmas present I could've asked for.

In a way, that was what Ella had given him.

Needing to see her, he went in search of her.

'She's writing up her notes from her last delivery in the office,' Jennie, one of their trainee midwives, told him. 'The baby had shoulder dystocia.'

Which meant extra forms, Oliver knew. 'Did everything go OK?'

'Yes.'

'Good.' He headed for the midwives' office. Ella was sitting at the desk; as usual, she'd dictated something first into her phone, and it looked as if she was listening to her notes and then typing them up a few words at a time. Oliver knew from reading Ella's file that she was dyslexic; he assumed that this was the way she'd learned to manage it, and it was also the reason why she wore coloured glasses when she was reading notes or sitting at a computer.

He rapped on the glass panel of the door to get

her attention, then opened it and leaned round it. 'Hi. I hear you just had a baby with shoulder dystocia.'

She nodded. 'There were absolutely no signs of it beforehand. The baby weighed three and a half kilograms and the mum didn't have gestational diabetes.'

'Prediction models aren't much help, as they're based on the baby's actual weight rather than the predicted weight, so don't blame yourself for it. In half of shoulder dystocia cases, we don't have a clue in advance, plus not all of them are big babies or from diabetic mothers,' Oliver said. 'How did it go?'

'Fine. As soon as I realised what was happening, I asked Jennie to get Charlie, the anaesthetist and the neonatal specialist. The McRoberts manoeuvre didn't quite work so I had to give her an episiotomy and guide the baby out, but the baby was fine and there's no sign of a brachial plexus injury. I'm going to keep an eye on Sophie—the mum—for postpartum haemorrhage.'

'Good job.' She looked so tired right now, Oliver thought. Having to concentrate on typing must be hard for her. 'Do you want a hand filling in the shoulder dystocia form?'

She narrowed her eyes at him. 'I'm not that hopeless, Oliver.'

And then the penny dropped. She obviously worried that people thought she was less than capable because of her dyslexia. Maybe in the past people had treated her as if she was stupid; that would explain why she'd overreacted to him buying the folic acid, because it had made her feel that he thought she was stupid.

'You're not hopeless at all, but you look tired,' he said, 'and filling in forms is a hassle even if you don't have to struggle with dyslexia as well.' He remembered what Ella's tutor said in her reference: ignore the exam results because Ella was an excellent midwife and could always tell you every last detail of a case. It just took her a lot longer than most to write it up. The exams must've been a real struggle for her, even if she'd been given extra time or the help of a scribe during the papers. And yet she'd never once given up. 'You could always dictate it to me and I'll type it up for you,' he suggested.

She narrowed her eyes even further. 'Would

you make the same offer to anyone else on your team?'

She was worried about him showing favouritism towards her because of the baby? 'Actually, yes, I would,' he said. 'That's the point. We're a team, at Teddy's. And I'm responsible for my team's well-being. Which includes you.' He pulled up a chair next to her, brought the keyboard in front of him and angled the screen so they could both see it. 'Right. Tell me what to type.'

Again she looked wary, and he thought she was going to argue with him; but then she nodded and dictated everything to him. Just as he'd expected, she was meticulous and accurate.

'Thank you,' she said when he'd finished typing.

'Any time. You know your stuff and you pay attention to our mums, so you made that really easy for me.' But she looked so tired, almost forlorn, and it worried him. He wanted to make things better. Now. He gave in to the impulse and rested his palm against her cheek. 'Tell me what you need.'

'Need?'

Her pupils were suddenly huge and his mouth went dry. Was she going to say that she needed him? Because, right now, he needed her, too. Wanted to hold her. Wanted to kiss her.

When she said nothing, he rubbed his thumb lightly against her skin. 'Cup of tea? Sandwich? Because I'm guessing the staff kitchen is a no-go area for you right now.'

'I'd love a cup of tea,' she admitted. 'And a sandwich. Anything really, really bland.'

'Give me five minutes,' he said. 'And, for the record, I'm not trying to be bossy. You've had a busy shift with a tough delivery, and I bet you haven't had the chance of a break today. I want to be there for you and our baby, Ella.'

He'd said the magic word, Ella thought as she watched Oliver leave the office. 'Our', not 'my'. So maybe she wasn't going to have to fight him for her independence.

He came back with the perfect cup of tea, a cheese sandwich and an apple that he'd cored and sliced for her. Ella felt her eyes fill with tears. 'Oh, Oliver.'

'Don't cry.'

But she couldn't stop the tears spilling over. He wrapped his arms round her, holding her close and making her feel cherished and protected, and that only made her want to cry more.

Hormones, that was all it was. And if someone came into the office and saw them, people might start to talk. Although Ella dearly wanted to stay in his arms, she wriggled free. 'Oliver. People are going to start gossiping if they see us like this.'

'No—they'll think you're tired after a long shift, and I'm doing exactly what I would for any colleague. Being supportive.'

'I guess.' She paused. 'I've got an appointment through for the scan.'

He went very still. 'Are you asking me to come with you?'

'If you want to.'

There was a brief flash of hunger in his eyes. Did that mean he wanted to be there, or did he think it was his duty? She didn't have a clue how he felt about her, and she wasn't ready to ask—just in case the answer was that he saw it as his duty.

'But if anyone asks why, it's because you're supporting your colleague,' she said. 'I'm not ready for the world to know about—well.' She shrugged. There wasn't an 'us'. What should she call it? A fling? A mistake? The most stupid thing she'd ever done in her life?

And yet the end result had been something she'd always thought was beyond her reach. The most precious gift of all. Something that made her heart sing every time she thought about the baby.

'Noted,' he said, his voice expressionless. 'What time?'

'Eleven.'

'I'll be there,' he said. 'Do you want me to meet you in the waiting area outside the ultrasound room, or here?'

'I think the waiting area would be best.' If they went together from here, their colleagues were bound to start speculating, and she really didn't want that. Not until she knew what was really happening between her and Oliver.

'All right.'

'I guess I'd better finish writing up my notes,' she said. 'And then I want to check on Sophie— the mum—to see how she and the baby are doing.

And I promised to give a hand with putting up the Christmas decorations in the reception area.'

'I'll let you get on, then.' For a moment, he looked as if he was going to say something else. Then he shook his head as if he'd changed his mind. 'I'll catch you later.'

CHAPTER FOUR

THE NEXT MORNING, Ella woke with butterflies in her stomach. The pregnancy test she'd taken had been positive; but as a midwife she knew that there were all manner of things that could go wrong over the next few weeks. One in four pregnancies ended in a miscarriage. And would the scarring in her Fallopian tubes have caused a problem with the baby?

She managed to force down a slice of toast and was sitting in the waiting room outside the ultrasound suite at five minutes to eleven, having drunk the requested one litre of water. There were Christmas cards pinned on the cork board in the reception area, and some of the tables had been moved to make way for a tree. All the couples sitting in the waiting room now were clearly looking forward to the following Christmas: the first Christmas with their new baby. Right now, Ella didn't know if she and the baby would still be here in Cheltenham with Oliver, or whether they'd be back in Ireland with her family, and it made her feel slightly melancholy.

Would Oliver be on time for the appointment? Or would he need to be in with a patient and have to miss the scan?

She reminded herself that it didn't matter if he couldn't be there; she could manage this perfectly well on her own. She tried to flick through one of the magazines left on the table to distract people who were waiting, but the paper was too shiny for her to be able to read the words easily.

And that was another worry: would her baby inherit her dyslexia? Ella knew that a daughter would have a one in four chance of inheriting the condition, and a son would have a three in four chance. She hated the idea that she could've passed on something that would cause her child difficulties in the future; though at least she was aware of what to look out for, so if necessary she'd be able to get help for her child much earlier than she'd received help, and her child wouldn't go through most of his or her education feeling as clumsy and stupid as Ella had.

She'd just put the magazine back on the table when she heard Oliver say, 'Good morning.'

She looked up and her heart skipped a beat. He really was beautiful: the walking definition of tall, dark and handsome. And she'd never reacted to someone as strongly as she reacted to Oliver.

'Good morning,' she said, trying to sound cool and collected and hoping that he didn't pick up how flustered he made her feel.

'Are you all right? Is there anything I can get you?'

'Thanks, but I'm fine. And, before you ask, yes, I've drunk all the water they asked me to.'

'Let's hope they're running on time so you're not uncomfortable for too long. May I?' He gestured to the chair next to her.

'Of course.' And how ridiculous it was that she longed for him to take her hand, the way that the partners of the other pregnant women in the waiting room seemed to have done. She had to remember that their relationship was limited to an unplanned and inconvenient shared status as a parent: they weren't a proper couple. They probably never would be. The best she could hope for was that Oliver would be there for the baby as he or she grew up. It would be stupid to dream that the man who'd held her yesterday afternoon when she'd cried, the man she was falling for just a little more each day, felt the same way about her. Yesterday he'd been kind, that was all.

A few minutes later, they were called into the ultrasound suite. As they walked into the dimly lit room, the sonographer said, 'Oh, Mr Darrington! I didn't expect to see you.' She looked speculatively at Ella. 'I didn't realise—'

'I'm supporting Ella,' Oliver cut in, 'as I'd support any member of my team whose family lives a long way away.'

'Oh, of course.' The sonographer blushed. 'I'm sorry for—well, making assumptions.'

Ella had wanted to keep everything just between the two of them, but at the same time she felt a prickle of hurt that Oliver hadn't acknowledged the fact that this was his baby, and had fudged it in a way so that he hadn't lied directly but had definitely misdirected the sonographer. She knew it was contrary and ridiculous of her to feel that way, and it was probably due to all the pregnancy hormones rushing round her system. How many times had she had to comfort a pregnant woman in their department who was upset for a totally irrational reason?

Following instructions, she lay on the couch and bared her stomach. The sonographer tucked tissue paper round Ella's clothes to stop them being covered in gel, then put radio-conductive gel on her stomach.

'It's warm,' Ella said in surprise. 'The gel is always cold if we do a scan on the ward.'

The sonographer smiled. 'It always is warm down here because of all the machinery heating up the room. I think it makes things a bit more comfortable for the mums.'

'I agree. We'll have to think of a way of doing that on the ward,' Ella said to Oliver.

The sonographer ran the head of the transceiver over Ella's stomach. 'Good. I can confirm there's just one baby here.'

Ella hadn't even considered that she might be having twins. She had no idea if twins ran in Oliver's family, but she could hardly ask him right then—not without adding to the hospital rumour mill.

'The baby's growing nicely,' the sonographer

said, and took some measurements on the screen. 'It's about thirteen millimetres long, so I'd say you're about seven and a half weeks.'

'That ties in with my dates,' Ella said.

'You can see the baby's head and body very clearly.' The sonographer turned the screen round to show them a bean-shaped blob; there was a flicker which Ella knew was the baby's heart-beat. And she was shocked by the rush of sheer emotion that burst through her at the very first sight of her baby.

'The baby's heart rate is one hundred and fifty beats per minute—which you'll know as a mid-wife is absolutely fine. It's too early to measure the fluid behind the neck for a Nuchal test, as we'd usually do that at about eleven weeks, but we can do a combined screening test for Down's then,' the sonographer said.

Ella only realised then that she'd been holding her breath, waiting to know that everything was all right and her fertility problems hadn't also caused a problem for the baby. 'Thank you. It's really good to know all's well.'

There was a knock on the door and another member of the ultrasound team put her head round the door. 'Sorry to interrupt—can I have a quick word?'

The sonographer went over for a brief discussion. 'I'm so sorry,' she said. 'I just need to pop next door for a moment. I'll be back very soon.'

'Not a problem,' Ella said, feeling a tug of sympathy for whoever was in the other ultrasound room. For the senior sonographer to be called in, it meant the team needed a second opinion on a potential complication.

As the door closed, Oliver took her hand. 'Our baby,' he said in wonder, looking at the screen. 'I've seen so many of these scans since I started working as an ob-gyn, and even performed a few of them myself, but this… This is special.' His voice sounded thick with emotion.

'I know.' It had affected Ella in the same way, and she was amazed by how strongly she felt. She'd only known about this baby for three days and it had turned her world upside down; but at the same time it was the most precious gift anyone could've given her and she was already bonding with the tiny being growing in her womb. She couldn't help tightening her fingers round his.

'Our baby, Ella,' he said again, his voice hoarse, and cupped her face with his free hand.

His touch sent a tingle through her. 'Oliver,' she whispered.

He dipped his head to kiss her; it was soft and sweet and full of longing.

When he broke the kiss, he pulled back just far enough so they could look into each other's eyes. Ella noticed that his pupils were huge. Was it because of the low light in the ultrasound room, or was it because he felt as emotional as she did right at that moment? Did he feel this same pull towards her that she felt towards him? Did they have a chance to make it as a couple—as a family?

'Ella,' he said softly, and kissed her again.

Her heart felt as if it had just done a somersault.

But then they heard the click of the door starting to open, and pulled apart again. Ella felt her cheeks burning, and really hoped that the sonographer hadn't seen anything—or, worse still, that she looked as if she'd just been thoroughly kissed.

Oliver looked both shocked and horrified. Ella could tell instantly that he was regretting the kiss and shrivelled a little inside. How stupid of her to hope that the kiss meant he felt something for her. Clearly he'd just got carried away by the rush of the moment.

'Sorry about that,' the sonographer said brightly. 'I guess as you work in Teddy's, Ella, you already know the answers to the kind of questions my mums normally ask, but is there anything you'd like to ask?'

Ella smiled. 'I'm not going to ask to know whether the baby's a girl or a boy, because apart from the fact I know it's way too early for you to be able to tell, it doesn't matter either way to me.' Though, she wondered, did it make a difference to Oliver? 'But would it be possible to have a photograph, please?'

'Sure. Let's see if we can get you a slightly less blurry picture,' the sonographer said with a smile. Once she'd got a picture she was happy with, she asked, 'How many copies do you need?'

'Two,' Ella said. 'How much are they?'

Before Oliver could embarrass them both by trying to pay, she took out her purse and handed over the money.

The photographs were printed while she wiped

her abdomen free of gel and restored order to her clothes.

'Thank you for your support, Oliver,' she said. 'I know you're really busy, so you don't have to hang around and wait for me.'

It was practically a dismissal. So Ella was obviously regretting their kiss, Oliver thought. And she was probably right. They could do with some space. He'd got carried away in the heat of the moment, overwhelmed by seeing the baby on the screen. Right now he needed to take a step back from Ella, metaphorically as well as literally.

'Thanks. I'll see you later on the ward,' he said.

But before he had a chance to leave the sonographer was called next door again.

'Ella,' he said, his voice low and urgent. 'What happened just now—it shouldn't have done. I apologise.'

'Uh-huh.' Her voice was very cool.

And he deserved that coolness. It was all his fault. 'I guess I lost my head a bit. It was the excitement of seeing the baby on the screen and hearing the positive news.'

'We both got carried away,' Ella agreed. 'It

won't happen again.' She gestured to the prints. 'I assume you'd like one of these?'

'I would.' It shocked him how very much he wanted the picture. *Their baby.* 'Thank you,' he said when she handed one to him.

'It's the least I could do.'

'I owe you—' he began.

'It's fine. A print of a scan isn't going to bankrupt me.'

That wasn't what he'd meant at all. 'Ella...' He sighed, seeing the determined set of her jaw. 'OK. I'll see you later. And thank you for the photograph.' He wasn't ready to share the news with anyone yet, but having the picture made everything so much more real. He tucked it into his wallet and left the room.

And he'd really have to get his head together.

He'd had no right to kiss her. The reason her fingers had tightened round his was purely because she was emotional about the baby. Seeing the little life they'd created, the strength of the baby's beating heart. That was all.

She wasn't in love with him.

And he wasn't in love with her, he told himself firmly. The attraction he felt towards her was because of the baby, rooted in responsibility rather than passion. He needed to be fair to her and leave her free to find someone else. Someone who hadn't put their heart in permafrost and would be able to give her the love she deserved.

But he'd meet every single one of his responsibilities towards the baby, and he needed to find a good working relationship with Ella, so their child never felt unwanted or a burden. They definitely needed to talk. Later—he really needed to gather his thoughts first.

Annabelle beckoned Ella into her office as she walked past. 'So how did it go?'

Ella beamed and took the scan picture from her purse. 'Look at this! I know, I know, it's too soon to see anything more than a bean-shaped blob.'

'It's gorgeous,' Annabelle said, looking slightly wistful.

Ella bit her lip. 'Oh, Annabelle, I'm sorry. I didn't mean to open up old wounds.' But she'd so wanted to share the picture with someone who'd understand how excited she was.

'You haven't upset me in the slightest.' Annabelle hugged her. 'I'm thrilled for you. Really, truly and honestly.'

'Thank you.' Ella tucked the picture back into her purse.

'So what's the situation between you and Oliver?' Annabelle asked.

'Complicated,' Ella admitted. Even though Annabelle was her best friend, Ella wasn't going to tell her about that kiss today. Oliver had apologised for it and said he'd got carried away in the heat of the moment and it was a mistake, so it'd be pointless for her to wish that it had meant anything more.

'Are you a couple, or not?'

'Not,' Ella said.

'Do you want to be?' Annabelle asked.

That was the crunch question. And the worst part was that Ella couldn't really answer it. 'I don't know. I like him, Annabelle—I like him a lot—but I don't want to lose my independence. I worked so hard to qualify as a midwife, and I hate the way Oliver just expects me to cut back on my shifts and do whatever he says. He obviously hasn't even thought about what it's going to do to my career.'

'I think,' Annabelle said, 'you need to talk to him.'

'You're right. I know,' Ella agreed.

'But, before that,' Annabelle said gently, 'you need to work out what you really want.'

And that was going to be the really hard part. Because right at that moment Ella wanted everything—and she knew that was way too much to ask.

That evening, when she got home, Ella video-called her parents.

'Is everything all right, darling?' Roisin O'Brien asked. 'You always call us on a Thursday, and today's only Tuesday.'

'I know. Mam, I have some news.'

Roisin beamed and asked hopefully, 'You're coming back to Ireland and going to work in the hospital in Limerick?'

Ella smiled. 'Mam, you know I love it here at Teddy's. No, it's not to do with work. Is Da there? Because I need to talk to you both together.'

'Is everything all right?' Roisin asked again.

'Yes.' And no, but she wasn't going to say that.

'Joe! Joe, our Ella's on the computer to talk to us,' Roisin called.

Joe appeared on Ella's screen, next to his wife. 'And how's my beautiful girl, then?'

Ella felt the tears well up. 'Oh, Da.'

Joe looked horrified. 'Ella? Whatever's the matter? I'll hop on the plane and be right over. You just say th—'

'No, Da, it's fine,' she cut in. She swallowed hard. 'Mam, Da—there isn't an easy way to say this, so I'll do what you always say and tell it to you straight. You're going to be grandparents.'

There was a stunned silence for a moment, and then Roisin said, 'But, Ella, the doctors in London said…' Her voice trailed off, and Ella knew what her mother didn't want to voice. The doctors in London had said Ella would never be able to have a child of her own.

'They got it wrong.' Ella picked up the scan photo and held it so her parents could see it. 'I had the scan today—I'm seven and a half weeks. You can't see a lot, just a bean shape, but the sonographer said everything looked fine and the baby's heart was beating just right.'

'We're going to be grandparents.' Joe and Roisin hugged each other.

'You're not angry with me?' Ella asked. 'Because—well, this wasn't supposed to happen?'

'So the baby wasn't planned. It doesn't mean he or she won't be loved to bits,' Roisin said. 'Lots of babies aren't planned. It's grand news, Ella. What about the baby's da? When do we get to meet him?'

Ella hadn't even considered that. 'I'm not sure,' she said carefully. 'It's complicated.'

'Do I need to come and talk to the lad and remind him of his responsibilities?' Joe asked, folding his arms.

'No, Da, and that's not why I called. I just wanted you both to know about the baby. It's early days and a lot of things could still go wrong—but I love you so much and I couldn't keep the news to myself any longer. Please don't say anything to anyone else in the family, not yet—not till I'm twelve weeks, OK?'

'All right. And we love you, too, Ella,' Roisin said. 'If you want us to move over to England to help you with the baby, you just say the word. Or if you want to come home, you've always got a home with us and so has the baby.'

'Oh, Mam.' Ella swallowed back the tears.

'So what does the young man in question have to say for himself?' Joe asked.

'He was at the scan with me today. He's very responsible,' Ella said, guessing what her father was worrying about. She smiled. 'He's trying to wrap me up in cotton wool as much as you do.'

'With about as much success, I'll bet,' Roisin said. 'You get your independent streak from your Granny O'Connor.'

'And your Granny O'Brien,' Joe added, not to be outdone.

Ella laughed. 'Oh, I miss you both so much.'

'You'll be home in a couple of weeks for Christmas,' Roisin said, 'and we can give you a proper hug then. Are you keeping well in yourself?'

'Just a bit of morning sickness.'

'You need crackers by your bedside,' Roisin began, then laughed. 'Hark at me trying to give a midwife advice on pregnancy.'

'You're my Mam,' Ella said. 'Of course you'll tell me, and when I get home you know I want to know *everything* about when you were pregnant with me.'

'She'll talk the hind leg off a donkey,' Joe said.

'As if you won't, too, Joe O'Brien,' Roisin teased back.

'You sort things out with your young man,' Joe said, 'and you bring him home with you for Christmas so we can give him a proper welcome to the family.'

'I'll try,' Ella said. And she knew her parents meant it. They'd definitely welcome Oliver. Her 'young man'. She couldn't help smiling. If only. 'I love you, Da. And you, Mam.'

'We love you, too,' Roisin said. 'Can we have a copy of that photo—our first picture of our grandbaby?'

'I'll scan it in and send it tonight,' Ella promised. 'As soon as we've finished our video call.'

'Good night, darling,' Roisin said. 'And you call us any time, you hear?'

'I hear. Love you,' Ella said, and ended the call.

It had made her homesick, and she was tearful again by the time she scanned in the photograph and emailed it over to her parents. Part of her wanted to call Oliver and ask him to come with her to Ireland for Christmas; but he probably already had plans. Plans that wouldn't include her. She'd just have to take this whole thing day by day, and hope that things would get easier between them.

Oliver brooded about the situation with Ella and the baby for the rest of Tuesday. It didn't help when he had a text from his mother, asking him if he could please confirm whether he was going to come to the drinks party at Darrington Hall on Thursday night.

He hadn't been to his parents' annual pre-Christmas drinks party for years. But maybe it was time he tried to thaw out his relationship with his family. Particularly as he was about to become a father.

How would his family react to the news? He had no idea. Would they expect him to settle down? Would they try to use the baby as an excuse to make him leave the hospital and spend his time working with his brother, instead of doing the job he'd trained for years and years to do? Would it be the thing that brought them back together again? Or would their awkward relationship be like a marriage under strain and crack even further under the extra pressure of a baby?

It was all such a mess.

It would help if he knew what Ella wanted. Did she regret what had happened between them? Or would she be prepared to try and make a life together?

He didn't have a clue.

And he didn't even know how to begin to ask.

CHAPTER FIVE

BY WEDNESDAY MORNING, the frustration was too much for Oliver. Usually he was self-contained, but right now he really needed to talk this over, preferably with someone he could trust to keep this to themselves.

The best person he could think of was Sebastian. Prince Sebastian Falco of Montanari had been one of his best friends since they'd met during Seb's first week at university, when Oliver had been nearing the end of his medical degree; they'd hit it off immediately, despite the four-year difference in their ages. Given his position as the heir to the kingdom of Montanari, Sebastian knew about the importance of privacy. And it didn't matter that Sebastian and Oliver hadn't actually seen each other for a few months; they always picked up their friendship exactly where they'd left off.

Oliver looked at the scan photograph again,

then picked up his mobile phone and called Sebastian's private number.

To his relief the prince answered immediately. 'Hello, Olly. How are you?'

All over the place. Not that Oliver was going to admit it. 'Fine, fine,' he fibbed. 'Seb, have I caught you in the middle of something, or do you have a few minutes?'

'I've probably got about ten minutes,' Sebastian said ruefully, 'and then I really do have to be in a meeting. It's good to hear from you, Olly. How are things?'

'Complicated,' Oliver said wryly.

'Would this be as in female complications?' Sebastian asked. 'Or is it the new job?'

'Both—and thank you for the case of champagne, by the way.'

'It's the least I could do,' Sebastian said. 'So what are these complications? I take it that's why you're ringing me—to get an impartial point of view?'

'And a bit of perspective.' Oliver blew out a breath. He really didn't know where to start. Or maybe he should just do the whole mixed-up lot at once. 'It's crazy at work, what with the winter vomiting virus wiping out half the staff, and Sienna's going on maternity leave any day now. And I'm going to be a father.'

There was silence on the other end of the line.

'Seb? Are you still there?'

Was his friend really that shocked by the news of Oliver's impending fatherhood? Oh, hell. That didn't bode well for his family's reaction. Sebastian was much more laid back than Oliver's parents.

'Sorry, Olly. Someone needed me for a second. You were saying, half of your department's having babies?' Sebastian asked.

'Not half of us—that's the virus wiping everyone out—though it does feel as if everyone's going on leave. Just Sienna. Obviously you know her from when she did the training at the hospital for you.'

'Yes. She did a good job—thank you for recommending her.'

There was something in Sebastian's voice that Oliver couldn't quite work out. Or maybe it wasn't the best line. He didn't always get great mobile phone reception in his office.

'So Sienna got married when she came back to England?' Sebastian asked.

'No, she's still single. But she knows we're all there for her and she's got a very willing rota of babysitters when the baby arrives. It's due somewhere around the beginning of February.'

'I see.' There was a pause. 'So you're going to be a dad. Should I be offering congratulations or commiserations?'

'Both,' Oliver said wryly. 'Though at least this one's definitely mine.'

'Not a repeat of Justine, then.'

Trust Sebastian to come straight to the point. It was one of the things that Oliver appreciated about his friend: his ability to focus on the important thing and cut through all the irrelevancies. 'No. And Ella's nothing like Justine. She's open and honest. And very independent.'

'So she won't let you boss her about.'

Oliver knew his friend was teasing him—or was he? Was he really as overbearing and bossy as Ella said he was?

'When's the baby due?' Sebastian asked.

'In seven and a half months.'

'It's very early days, then.'

'Yes. Ella only told me a few days ago. She had the dating scan yesterday. Seeing the baby's heart beating on the screen...' It had been a real game-changer. Because now everything was real. *His baby.* And he wanted to be a much better father than his own father had been.

Yet wasn't he making the same mistakes? Insisting that everything should go his way? It was a knee-jerk reaction to the way Justine had behaved—and Ella deserved better.

'So what's the complication with the baby's mum?' Sebastian asked.

Trust the prince to ask the awkward question. 'It's tricky. I'm not her direct boss, but I'm the Assistant Head of the Department.'

'Well, it wouldn't be the first workplace romance in history.'

When Oliver didn't reply, Sebastian continued, 'I assume it *is* a romance?'

'Yes and no.' Oliver sighed. 'I admit, I've been attracted to her since the moment I met her. She's gorgeous—all soft curves and red hair and green eyes.'

'The way you describe her makes her sound

like a Picasso painting,' Sebastian commented dryly.

Oliver laughed. 'Hardly. It's not just how she looks—I'm not that shallow. She's *nice*. I can be myself with her. But you know I don't do relationships. So I've kept it platonic.'

'Obviously something changed, or you wouldn't be preparing for fatherhood in seven and a half months' time,' Sebastian pointed out.

'I danced with her at the annual Hallowe'en charity ball. Then I gave her a lift home.' Which sounded pathetic. 'I meant to see her safely indoors and leave, but she invited me in for coffee. And then I just gave in to the urge to kiss her, and...' Oliver sighed. 'I guess one thing led to another.'

'How does she feel about you?'

Good question. One Oliver had been asking himself rather a lot, and he hadn't quite worked out the answer. 'I don't honestly know. Obviously there's something there between us, or we wouldn't be in the position we're in now. But the baby has complicated things a bit. I don't know whether she wants me for *me*,' he said, 'or if she wants me for the baby's sake.'

'Have you tried asking her?'

'No—because, if I'm honest, it's the same for me. I don't know if I want to be with her because I want her, or because I feel responsible for the baby.' Though he wasn't going to tell Sebastian about the kiss during the scan. That complicated things even more. Had they both been caught up in the moment, the excitement of seeing the little life on screen? Or were they both trying to deny the inevitable? Were they meant to be together?

And then there was the issue of why she'd been so sure that he hadn't needed to use contraception. He still hadn't got to the bottom of that. He didn't think Ella was a gold-digger, but there was definitely something she was keeping from him, and he hadn't found the right way to ask her about it without causing a fight. 'Right now, everything's mixed up.'

'I guess only time will tell,' Sebastian said. 'Just make sure you keep the lines of communication open.'

Oliver knew that was sound advice. 'I will.'

'Have you told your family yet?'

'No. It's too early.'

'Fair enough.' Sebastian paused. 'Does Ella know about your family?'

The crunch question. Sebastian knew Oliver kept his background quiet at work, and why. 'No,' Oliver admitted.

'You're going to have to tell her at some point. And them. Especially if she's going to be a part of your future.'

'I know.' He'd been thinking about that. He needed to introduce Ella to his family; and, given that they seemed to be reaching out to him right now, maybe their attitude towards his career might have mellowed and they'd accept him for who he was rather than who they wanted him to be. 'My mother wants me to go to the annual Darrington pre-Christmas cocktail party.'

'Then go,' Sebastian said.

'You know I haven't been for years.' He hated all that meet-and-greet stuff.

'Things are different now. You need to introduce Ella to them. And,' Sebastian counselled, 'a party where there are a lot of people around would be a useful way of doing that.'

'You mean, it's in public so my parents will

have to behave impeccably, and there will be enough other people there to dilute them?'

'I didn't say that.' But Oliver could almost hear the smile in his friend's voice, because they both knew what his family was like. Appearances mattered to the Darringtons. Sebastian, being a prince, was perfect friend material in their eyes. Ella came from a very different background, and it probably wouldn't go down well.

Oliver didn't need his parents to approve of Ella. Their relationship—if they could make it a real relationship—was just between the two of them. But he was starting to realise that family was important. Was there a place for his family in his future? Could they learn from the mistakes of the past and build some bridges?

'Olly, I really have to go,' Sebastian said. 'Sorry. I'll call you back when I'm out of my meeting.'

'I'll probably be in a meeting then myself, or in Theatre,' Oliver said. 'But you don't need to call me back, Seb. I think you've already helped me work out the best way forward. Thank you.'

'Any time. Good luck,' Sebastian said. 'And keep me posted on how things go.'

'I will. And thanks again.'

Once he'd put the phone down, Oliver texted his mother.

Confirm will be there on Tomorrow. May I bring a guest? There's someone I'd like you to meet.

The reply came back.

Of course. Look forward to meeting her.

Grilling her, more like, he thought. He definitely wouldn't leave Ella on her own at Darrington Hall. Even if she did protest that he was wrapping her in cotton wool.

'Mummy, look, it's Santa!' The little boy tugged at his mum's hand and pointed to the room on the other side of the floor, and Ella couldn't help smiling at the excitement on his face.

'Santa'—often one of the consultants in a borrowed suit—paid a brief visit to Teddy's every Wednesday afternoon in December, to see the siblings of all the new babies on the ward. The Friends of the Hospital group had raised money for gifts appropriate for different ages—a soft toy, colouring pencils and a pad, or a reading book—and it helped to make the older siblings feel that they were still special despite the new arrival in the family.

So who was it today? Oliver? Max?

Definitely not Oliver, because a couple of minutes later he came striding along the corridor. He paused in the doorway when he saw Ella, and smiled. 'OK?'

Ella nodded, and glanced back at the mum she'd been checking over. She was busy with the baby and talking to her toddler, so Ella stepped out for a second. 'You?'

'Yeah.'

'I wondered if you were, um, helping our friend in the red suit.'

He smiled. 'That would be next week.' For a moment, he took her hand and squeezed it. 'Next year, our baby will see Santa.'

His voice was low enough so that nobody else would've heard. And that touch, combined with the expression in his eyes and what he'd just said, sent a thrill right through her. Especially when he added, 'And I can't wait. I know five months is still a bit young, but…'

Did that mean he wanted to take the baby to

see Santa on his own? Or did he mean the three of them as a family? Not that she could ask. Yesterday, he'd kissed her; but then he'd said it was a mistake. Right now they seemed to be taking one step forward and two steps back.

Or maybe this was her chance to sound him out a little more. 'The year after will be better,' she said. 'Because by then the baby will be talking and know what's going on.'

'We're so getting a train set for the second Christmas,' he said. 'Whether we have a girl or a boy. Wooden trains are the best fun.'

And she could just see him kneeling on the floor with their baby, helping their little one put the train tracks together. Her heart constricted. But would she be there with him?

'You're going to be an amazing mum,' he said. 'Singing nursery rhymes and telling stories with all the voices.'

He'd been thinking about the future, then? Just the baby, or about them too? She let herself get carried away with the fantasy that it was all of them. 'And you're going to be the dad who does all the scary stuff—the highest slide in the park, pushing the swings as fast as they'll go.'

'That sounds good to me,' he said. 'But not that scary. I'll always keep my own safe.'

Right at that second she wasn't sure whether he was talking about the baby or her. And she so wanted it to be both of them.

'Ella—can I borrow you for a second?' Jennie, their trainee midwife, asked.

Oh, help. Ella really hoped that Jennie hadn't overheard any of that conversation.

'Sure,' she said, keeping her fingers crossed that she didn't sound flustered. 'I'll just let my mum know I'll be with you for a little while before I finish writing up her notes. I think they're next for Santa, so they won't miss me. Catch you later, Oliver.'

'Later,' he agreed with a smile.

It was just a work pleasantry, that was all, she reminded herself. She might not even see him again before the end of her shift. But at least they hadn't been fighting. That had to be a start.

Once Ella had helped Jennie and finished writing up her notes, she was called to the birthing suite for another delivery. This was the best job in the world, she thought, watching the little family in front of her: the dad with tears of pride and joy in his eyes, the mum looking tired but radiant, and the baby cuddled up between them. To be able to share these first few precious minutes of a new life was so amazing.

The delivery had been free from complications, the baby had had a perfect Apgar score, and now the three of them were settled back on the ward.

Would Oliver cry when their baby arrived, the way this baby's dad had cried with sheer joy? Or would he be perfectly cool, calm and collected? Given what he'd said to her when Santa came onto the ward, she had a feeling it would be the former. And he had talked about next Christmas, so it sounded as if he wanted to be part of the baby's life.

There was still a lot they weren't saying to each other, but at least they weren't arguing. So maybe they'd manage to work things out between them.

She left the little family to bond and went to write up her notes in the quiet of the office.

She was halfway through when there was a rap on the door. She looked up to see Oliver standing in the doorway.

'Can I have a word?' he asked.

Her heart skipped a beat as she thought about the way he'd kissed her in the ultrasound room yesterday; but then she remembered how quick he'd been to dismiss it as a simple reaction to seeing the baby and hearing the good news. Despite what he'd said to her earlier today about their baby and next Christmas, they hadn't actually resolved their relationship. And she had to be objective about this. Oliver Darrington might be the father of her baby, but he wasn't in love with her. She'd be a fool to dream it would ever happen. She damped down the flare of desire. 'Sure,' she said, as coolly as she could. 'Though I'm in the middle of writing up the birth notes.'

'Did it go well?'

'Very. There were no complications, and I left the new mum and dad bonding with their little girl.' She smiled. 'The dad cried when she was born. It was so lovely to see how happy they were.' And oh, she had to stop talking. The last thing she wanted was for Oliver to guess how she was feeling. 'You wanted something?'

'Yes. What are you doing tomorrow?'

'Cleaning my flat,' she said, 'as it's my day off.

And I really ought to do a bit of Christmas shopping. I'm a bit behind, this year.'

'Are you busy in the evening?' he asked.

'Why?'

'Because my parents are having a cocktail party.' He looked awkward. 'I wondered if you'd like to come with me.'

He wanted her to meet his parents?

Ella stared at him in surprise. 'Are you sure? I mean... They didn't invite me.'

'They have now. I asked if I could bring you.'

So he'd already talked to his family about her? Had he told them about the baby, despite the fact he'd suggested she shouldn't tell anyone until she was past the first trimester?

She pushed down the rising panic. Cocktail party, he'd said. She didn't know anyone who actually held cocktail parties. She knew that Oliver had quite a posh accent. But how posh exactly were they? Would she fit in?

As if he'd guessed what she was thinking, he said, 'It's not a big deal. Just a drinks party they hold every year before Christmas.'

It was an annual event? That sounded even scarier. 'It sounds a little bit fancy,' she said.

Oliver's face shuttered. 'All right. So you don't want to meet my family.'

She shook her head. 'No, that's not what I meant, Oliver. I was just thinking that it sounds like quite a big party and your parents will be busy. Wouldn't it be better if I met them at something a bit quieter and more low-key rather than a big event?' And something she could escape from more easily. 'Like, I don't know, meeting at a café in town for a cup of tea?'

'It's probably better,' he said, 'if there are a lot of people there.'

That sounded ominous. Did that mean he thought they were going to hate her, especially when they found out about the baby? Or did they already know about the baby and they weren't pleased?

Clearly her worries showed in her face because he said, 'What I mean is that my family can be a little bit pushy—I guess that's where I get my overbearing streak. I think the first time you meet them will be better if they're a bit diluted. They're the problem, not you.'

That didn't calm Ella's worries in the slightest. Particularly as she knew that her own family would welcome Oliver warmly when she introduced him to them. They'd draw him straight into the middle of things and treat him as if they'd known him for years and years. Her father had already said they wanted to welcome him to the family.

Clearly Oliver's family was very different, and she'd have to tread very carefully.

'Have you told them about the baby?' she asked.

'Not yet.'

'Because they won't approve of me?' The question burst out before she could stop it.

'Because,' he said, 'it's still early days. I'd prefer to wait until you're safely through the first trimester before we tell my family about the baby.'

That was sensible; though it made her feel guilty that everyone in the department already knew. It felt wrong to be sharing this with their colleagues and not Oliver's family, especially as she'd already shared the news with her own family. But how could she explain that? 'OK.' She paused. 'So what do I wear? If it's a big cocktail party...'

'I'll buy you a dress,' Oliver said.

She frowned. 'No—and that's not why I asked. Is the dress I wore to the masked ball suitable?'

'Yes, but I can b—' he began.

'No,' she cut in. 'You really don't need to buy me a dress, Oliver. It's a total waste to buy something you're only ever going to wear to one thing.'

He sighed. 'I'm being bossy again?'

She nodded.

'Got it,' he said. 'Will you allow me to drive you to the party?'

'Yes, but only because you know the way.'

'All right.' His grey eyes were unreadable. 'I'll pick you up tomorrow, then.'

'What time do I need to be ready?'

'The party starts at half-past seven, and it takes about an hour to get there. So I'll pick you up at half-past six.'

'I'll be ready. Should I have dinner first?'

'There will be nibbles there—but yes, I'd say grab a sandwich or something before I pick you up,' Oliver said.

Ella noticed that he didn't suggest eating together first, and pushed down the feeling of hurt. After all, she'd already accused him of being bossy. He'd probably thought she'd bite his head off if he suggested it. 'All right. I'll see you to-morrow then.'

She watched him walk out of the door. Had he just asked her on a date of sorts? Was he thinking about trying to make a go of things between them, and introducing her to his family was the first step? Or was this some kind of test she needed to pass?

'You're overthinking it, you numpty,' she told herself crossly. She knew Oliver didn't play games. He was simply introducing her to his family. Not as the mother of his child, but as... She didn't quite know what as, but it was most likely he'd say she was his colleague or maybe his friend. And then, when he'd worked out how his family reacted to her, he'd find the right way to break the news about the baby. It was nothing to worry about.

'We're going to be just fine,' she said, resting her hand where her bump wasn't even visible yet. 'If they don't like us—well, that's their problem, and we'll deal with it if and when we have to.'

CHAPTER SIX

DESPITE HER BRAVE intentions of the night before, Ella spent Thursday feeling really nervous. What would Oliver's parents be like? Would they accept her? He'd said that his relationship with them was complicated. Would the baby make things worse? Or was he hoping that the baby would be a bonding point?

But then again, how many people thought that having a baby would paper over the cracks in their relationship, only to find instead that the pressure of having a newborn made the cracks burst wide open? And that would be true of any family relationship, not just that of the baby's parents.

She tried not to think about it too much while she cleaned her flat, and it made her feel slightly better when Annabelle sent her a text during her break on the ward.

KATE HARDY 163

Good luck for tonight. Am sure O's parents will love you.

Then she went into Cheltenham to do her Christmas shopping, and all her fears came back. Everywhere she looked, she seemed to see new mums proudly pushing a pram with their partners by their side.

Tears pricked her eyelids. She *missed* her parents. And she knew they'd both be doting grandparents, always ready with a cuddle and a story. Would Oliver's parents feel the same way about the baby? Or would it make their strained relationship with Oliver more difficult?

Plus it was still very early days in her pregnancy—especially given the complications of her own medical history, which she hadn't yet felt comfortable enough to share with Oliver. The sonographer hadn't said anything, but what if there was a cyst on her other ovary? What if it grew during the pregnancy and she ended up needing an operation to remove it? She knew that kind of operation wasn't usually done until halfway through the pregnancy, to protect the baby—but what if the cyst ruptured, like the other one had?

'Stop it. You're borrowing trouble, and you know that's stupid,' she told herself crossly.

It had to be hormones making her all tearful and miserable like this, because Ella had never been a whiner. Even on days when the pain of her endometriosis had made it hard for her to crawl out of bed, she'd tried her best to pretend that everything was just fine.

And she needed to be on top form tonight, all smiley and cheerful, so Oliver's family would like her.

Oliver.

Should she get him a Christmas present? They weren't in a relationship exactly, but he was her baby's father. Though Ella didn't have a clue what to buy him. He never shared anything personal at work. Although she knew from the night of the Hallowe'en ball that he liked piano music, she didn't know what he already owned. And she didn't want to buy him something bland and impersonal like a bottle of wine.

She shook herself. She'd worry about that later. For now, she needed to think about meeting his family and hoping she could make them like her.

The shopping and the cleaning took it out of her,

and she ended up falling asleep over her books. She had only just enough time to get ready, grab a sandwich and do her hair and make-up before Oliver arrived at precisely half-past six.

'You look lovely,' he said.

'Thank you.' So did he, in a dinner jacket and bow tie—just as he'd worn to the ball. Evening dress suited him.

And she remembered exactly what it had felt like to slide that shirt off his shoulders and trace his pectoral muscles with her fingertips—and how it had felt when he'd unzipped the dress she was wearing right now...

Oh, help. She really had to keep her imagination and her memory under strict control. Tonight she needed to be on her best behaviour—and that didn't mean doing what she really wanted to do most at that moment and kissing Oliver until they were both dizzy with need and ended up back in her bed. Especially as she wasn't sure at all how he felt about her.

Hormones, she reminded herself. This is all just hormones rushing round and I need to be sensible. 'Um—would you like a drink?' she asked.

'Tea would be good, thanks.' He looked slightly wary. 'I need to talk to you about something.'

This didn't sound good. 'Come in and sit down.' She busied herself making tea; he didn't say anything, which made her feel even more awkward. But she wasn't a coward; she'd face this head on. 'What did you want to talk about?'

'My family,' he said, surprising her. 'I know I don't have to ask you to keep this confidential.'

Because he trusted her? That was a good thing. If he was going to tell her why his relationship with his parents was tricky, it might stop her accidentally making things worse tonight. 'Of course I'll keep whatever you tell me to myself,' she said, wanting to reassure him.

'I don't mention my family at work,' he said, 'because I want people to see me for who I am, not whose son I am.'

She frowned. 'Your dad's famous?'

He coughed. 'My father's the Earl of Darrington.'

It took her a while to process it. 'You mean your family's like a real-life version of the one in *Downton Abbey*?'

'Yes.'

She stared at him, not quite able to believe this. She'd known Oliver was posh, but *this* posh? Oh, help. She didn't quite know how to deal with this.

'So should I have been calling you Lord Darrington all these months?' she asked carefully.

'No. I'm not the oldest son, so I'm just the Hon Oliver Darrington,' he said. 'Addressed as plain Mr Darrington, just as you're addressed as Miss O'Brien.'

'Ms,' she corrected. And as for his 'just the Hon'—she didn't know anyone else who was an Hon. And then a really nasty thought struck her. 'Oliver, you don't think I'm a gold-digger, do you? Because I had absolutely no idea you were—well, from that kind of background.'

Shock spread across his face. 'Of course you're not a gold-digger, Ella. Apart from the fact that nobody at work knows about my background, you're completely open and honest.'

That wasn't quite true. She hadn't been totally honest with him about her past, because she hadn't wanted him to pity her. Guilt trickled through her—but the worry was uppermost. 'So this party tonight's going to be really, really posh?'

He grimaced. 'A bit. And I understand if you'd

rather not go. I probably should have told you when I asked you to come with me.'

'I wish you had, because at least then I could've maybe found something more suitable to wear while I was out shopping today.' She gestured to her dress. 'Everyone's going to take one look at me and know this was a sale bargain and probably cost less than their underwear. I'm not going to fit in. And your parents are going to think I'm just after your money. Which,' she added, just in case he was under any kind of misapprehension on that score, 'I'm not.'

Oliver came to stand before her and pulled her to her feet. 'Ella O'Brien, you look beautiful. Nobody whose opinion matters will think anything about what you're wearing other than the fact that you look lovely. You're more than good enough to hold your own at any party, whether it's the pub quiz between Teddy's and the Emergency Department, or the ballroom at Darrington Hall full of...' He spread his hands. 'Well.'

'Lords and ladies?' she asked wryly.

'Not all of them will have a title,' he said. 'But yes. You're more than good enough, Ella.'

There was a slash of colour across his cheeks,

telling her that he felt really strongly about this. He really did believe that she could fit in.

And then, the expression in his eyes changed. Turned from fierceness to heat. Achingly slowly, he dipped his head to brush his mouth against hers. There was a sweetness to his kiss, just like when he'd kissed her in the ultrasound room, and Ella found herself melting against him and returning his kiss.

'You're wearing the same dress you wore that night,' Oliver whispered against her mouth. 'That night we made love. The night we made our baby.'

His hand slid down to rest protectively over her abdomen, and Ella's pulse speeded up a notch. On impulse, she rested her hand over his, and he moved slightly so that her fingers were entwined with his, united and protective.

'And you're wearing that suit,' she whispered back. 'I can remember taking your shirt off.'

His eyes darkened. 'Ella. I can't stop thinking about that night. How it felt to be with you.' He stole another kiss. 'The scent of your hair. The feel of your bare skin against mine.' His teeth grazed her earlobe as he whispered, 'I haven't stopped wanting you. And now you're carrying our baby, it makes me want to...'

'Yes.' Oh, yes. She wanted it, too. That shared closeness she'd only ever known with him. Except this time it would be different. Because they'd created a new life, and when he explored her he'd notice the tiny, subtle changes. And she knew he'd tell her about every single one in that amazingly sexy posh voice.

Right now her skin felt too tight. Especially when he kissed her again, pulling her close against him, and her hardened nipples rubbed against him.

'Oliver,' she breathed.

But, when Ella felt Oliver's fingers brush the skin on her back as he began to slide the zip of her dress slowly downward, common sense kicked back in. Yes, she wanted to make love with him. Desperately. But she was supposed to be going to meet his family. She needed to make a good impression. Turning up late, looking as if she'd just had sex, with her mouth all swollen and her hair all mussed—that most definitely wouldn't be the right impression.

'Oliver. We *can't*. We're going to be late.'

He stroked her face. 'Or we can skip the party.'

'But your parents are expecting us. It's rude not to turn up.'

'I know. But I can say I was held up at work.'

'Which isn't true.'

'It's a white lie.'

It sounded as if he didn't want to go to the party, and not just because he wanted to carry her to her bed. She narrowed her eyes at him. 'What else aren't you telling me, Oliver?'

He sighed. 'Nothing, really.'

'You said things were strained between you and your parents. Is not turning up going to make things worse? Or will it be worse when they meet me and realise I'm not from your world?'

He rested his palm against her cheek. 'Trust you to hit the nail on the head. OK. Let's just say that they had other plans for me, so they're not brilliantly happy that I went into medicine.'

She couldn't understand why. 'But you're Assistant Head of Department at a ridiculously young age. Doesn't that tell them how good you are at what you do?'

'I didn't actually tell them about the promotion,' he admitted.

'Why? For pity's sake, Oliver, aren't they massively proud of you? Because they ought to be! You're really good at your job. What you do is *important*.'

Ella was batting Oliver's corner for him, and it made him feel odd. He'd never, ever dated anyone who'd backed him like that before. With Justine, he was always the one doing the protecting; but Ella was different. She was his equal.

Strictly speaking, he and Ella weren't actually dating. But there was more to their relationship than just the shared unexpected parenthood. And the fact that she was backing him like this... Maybe she was the one that he could trust with his heart. The one who'd see him for who he really was. 'You really think that?' he asked.

She put her hands on her hips and rolled her eyes at him. 'Oliver Darrington, you're the one who makes the difference in a tricky birth between someone having a baby, and someone losing their baby. You've saved babies and you've saved their mums, too. And if that's not more important than—than—' She waved a hand in disgust. 'Than having a title, then I don't know what is.'

Even with her lipstick smudged and her hair slightly mussed from their shared kiss, Ella looked magnificent. A pocket Amazonian.

'You,' he said softly, 'are amazing. Never let anyone else ever tell you otherwise.'

'So are you,' Ella said fiercely. 'So we're going to this party, and your family can see that for themselves.'

'Right.' He stole another kiss. 'Though you might want to put some more lipstick on and fiddle with your hair.'

'Give me two minutes,' Ella said.

And she was ready in the time it took him to wash up their undrunk mugs of tea.

Ella didn't manage to get much more out of Oliver about his family on the journey, other than that his older brother Ned was married to Prue and they had three girls. Her bravado dimmed a bit when Oliver explained that Ned was the heir to the earldom and he was the 'spare' until Ned and Prue had a son—particularly when she worked out that if Ned and Prue didn't have a son and something happened to Ned, Oliver would be the future Earl of Darrington; and then if her baby was a boy he would be the heir, which would make her the mother of an earl. Her nerves threatened to outweigh the bravery completely when Oliver drove down the long, narrow driveway lined with trees and she saw just how big Darrington Hall was. Her worries grew as he parked his car among what she recognised as Rolls-Royces and Bentleys. No way could she fit into this kind of world. If his parents didn't approve of his job, they'd approve even less of her.

He helped her from the car, and led her up the steps to the porticoed entrance. They were greeted at the door by a butler wearing white gloves, who took their coats. 'Good to see you again, Master Oliver,' he said, dipping his head in acknowledgement.

'Thank you, Benson,' Oliver said with a smile.

'Everyone's in the ballroom, Master Oliver,' the butler said.

'Thanks, Benson. This way, Ella,' Oliver said.

The reception hall was massive, with a huge sweeping staircase, polished wooden floors, a carpet that looked as if it was an antique worth hundreds of thousands of pounds, and a whole gallery of portraits in heavy gold frames.

'Are they...?' Ella asked, gesturing to them.

'The Earls of Darrington, yes. My father's the one over there.'

The newest portrait. The current Earl had a stern face, Ella thought. And he was wearing very formal dress; she imagined it was what he'd wear in the House of Lords.

He really, really wasn't going to approve of her.

There were serving staff dressed in black and white, carrying silver trays filled with glasses of champagne or exquisite canapés. The trays looked as if they were real silver, Ella thought, rather than the polished chrome used in a restaurant.

She felt even more out of place when they walked into the ballroom itself. Again, the room was massive, with wooden-panelled walls, a huge marble fireplace, more oil paintings in heavy frames and the most enormous crystal chandelier. There was a baby grand piano in the corner of the room, and the man sitting on the piano stool was playing soft jazz, not quite loudly enough to disturb the hum of conversation. And the only time she'd seen a Christmas tree that big was in one of the posh London stores. It looked professionally decorated, too—not like the Christmas trees in her family, strewn with decorations made over the years at school by each child. All the reds and golds of the different decorations matched, and the spacing between baubles was so precise that someone must've used a tape measure.

But then Oliver tucked her hand firmly in the crook of his arm and was walking her over towards a couple at the other side of the room.

'Olls! I thought Mama had been at the sherry when she said you were turning up tonight,' the man said, clapping him on the back.

Even without the words, Ella would've guessed that this was Oliver's brother, because they looked so alike.

'Very funny, Ned. I'd like you to meet Ms Ella O'Brien. Ella, this is my elder brother Ned, and how he managed to persuade lovely Prue here to marry a scoundrel like him is beyond me,' Oliver said, laughing.

'I—um—how do you do, Lord Darrington?' Ella said awkwardly, holding out a hand, really hoping that she'd got the etiquette right. Or should she be curtsying to him? She only just resisted the urge to kick Oliver very hard on the ankle for not giving her anywhere near enough information about how to deal with this.

Viscount Darrington shook her hand. 'Delighted to meet you, Ms O'Brien, or may I call you Ella?'

She could see where Oliver got his charm from, now. 'Ella's fine,' she said, cross with herself for squeaking the words.

'And you must call me Ned,' he said with a warm smile.

'And I'm Prue. We don't stand on ceremony, whatever nonsense Olls might have told you,' Viscountess Darrington said. Then she shook her head in exasperation. 'Did he not even let you get a drink, first? That's terrible. Olls, your manners are shocking. Come with me, Ella— let's leave these heathens to sort themselves out. What would you like? Some champagne?'

'Thank you,' Ella said, 'but I'm on an early shift tomorrow, so I'd rather not be drinking alcohol tonight.'

'Let's sort you out with something soft, then,' Prue said with a smile. 'And I'm sure we have you to thank for Olls actually coming to the party. He normally wriggles out of it.'

'I...um...' Ella didn't know what to say.

'And it's really bad of him to drop you right in the middle of this without any warning,' Prue said. 'This place is a bit overwhelming, the first time you see it—and with all these people about it's even more intimidating.' She shook her head again and tutted. 'I'm so sorry, Ella. If he'd actually told us he was bringing you, I'd have suggested meeting you in Cheltenham for lunch first—somewhere quiet, where we could have had a proper chat and got to know each other a bit before tonight.'

Ella really hadn't expected Oliver's family to be so welcoming, not after he'd said things were strained between them. But Prue Darrington was a real sweetheart, and Ella began to feel just the tiniest bit better about being here.

'I think the invitation was all a bit last-minute,' she said.

Prue rolled her eyes. 'The Darrington men are all the same—they're total rubbish at communicating. But I'm so glad you've come. It's lovely to meet you. And I do like your necklace. It's so pretty.'

Ella wasn't sure whether Prue really meant the compliment or was just being kind, but she was grateful that at least someone here wasn't looking down on her. 'Thank you.'

'I take it you work with Olls?' Prue asked.

Ella nodded. 'I'm a midwife.'

'What a wonderful job to have—to see those first precious moments of life,' Prue said.

'I love it,' Ella confided shyly. 'Oliver says you have three girls?'

'We do. Rose, Poppy and Lily—aged five, three and thirteen months respectively.'

'They're very pretty names,' Ella said.

Prue grinned. 'That's the great thing about having a girl Darrington. You actually get to choose her name yourself.'

Ella blinked. 'You mean, if you'd had a boy, you wouldn't have been able to choose his name, even though you're his mum?'

'The firstborn boy is *always* Edward.' Prue winked. 'Though if we ever have a son, I plan to rebel and always refer to him by his middle name.'

As they walked by a towering floral display,

Ella discovered that the heavy perfume of lilies brought on a rush of morning sickness.

'Are you all right?' Prue asked.

'Fine,' Ella fibbed.

'No, you're not. You've gone green. Come on, let's get you a glass of water and somewhere quiet to sit down.'

Prue was as good as her word, and Ella felt better when she'd had a sip of water.

Prue lowered her voice. 'So how far along are you?'

'I don't know what you mean,' Ella said, inwardly horrified that Prue had guessed her secret already.

'Ella, you're a midwife and I have three girls. When someone female goes green at the scent of lilies, either they have hay fever—in which case they'll start sneezing the place down within two seconds—or...' Prue squeezed Ella's hand. 'If it makes you feel any better, I'll tell you a secret. If the party had been last week instead of tonight, I would've turned green as well at the scent of those lilies.'

'You're...?'

Prue nodded, and lifted a finger to her lips.

'Ned and I promised each other not to tell any-one until I'm twelve weeks.'

And that gave Ella the confidence to admit the truth. 'Me, too. Almost eight weeks. But please don't tell anyone,' she said. 'Not even Ned.'

'OK. I promise. But you have to make the same promise,' Prue said. 'You can't even tell Olls for the next three weeks.'

'I promise,' Ella said.

'But this is such fabulous news,' Prue said. 'Our babies will be practically the same age. Which means they'll have a great time romping around this place together.'

'I used to play with my cousins all the time, when I was young,' Ella said. And she loved the idea of her baby having a built-in family like this, just the way that she had.

'My cousins all lived too far away for us to see them that often. And I was the only one, so I was determined to have lots and lots of children,' Prue said. 'Ned's desperate for a boy. Not because of the entailment and all that nonsense about a son and heir, but because he says he's going to need some support when the girls are teens and we

all have PMT at the same time and he'll be ter-
rified of us.'

Ella couldn't help laughing. She really, really liked Oliver's sister-in-law, and she had the
feeling they were going to become good friends.
'I bet the girls wrap him round their little fingers.'

'They do,' Prue confirmed. 'And you should
hear him read them a bedtime story. It's so cute.'

Would Oliver be like that as a father, totally
involved with their baby?

Then again, she and Oliver weren't a proper
couple—despite the way he'd kissed her tonight.

Ella pushed the thought away as Ned and Oliver came over to join them.

'I wondered where you'd both disappeared to,'
Ned said.

'Sorry. I just needed to sit down for a moment,' Ella said. 'It's been a crazy shift at work
today. I had a mum with a water birth, and then a
scary one where the cord was wrapped round the
baby's neck. Luckily there was a happy ending
in both cases.' It wasn't strictly true—although
that particular shift had happened, it had been a

fortnight ago rather than today—but she hoped that the story would keep Ned off the scent.

'We really have to circulate, darling, or Mama will be on the warpath,' Ned said to Prue with a grimace. 'Ella, please excuse us—but do make sure you find us later, because I'd love to get to know you a bit better. And make sure Prue has your mobile number so we can arrange dinner.'

'I will,' Ella promised.

'Are you really all right?' Oliver asked when his brother and sister-in-law had gone.

'Yes.' She gave him a wan smile. 'The lilies got to me.'

'Right.' Understanding filled his gaze.

'Sorry for telling the fib about work.'

'No. I understand. You needed to—otherwise you'd have had to tell them.'

And she'd already told Prue, she thought, feeling guilty. 'I like your brother and sister-in-law,' she said.

'They're good sorts,' Oliver said. He looked her straight in the eye. 'Are you feeling up to meeting my parents?'

Even the idea of it made butterflies stampede through her stomach. It was so important that she got this right and made a good impression, for Oliver's sake. But Prue and Ned had been so nice and welcoming. Surely Oliver's parents would be the same, even if things were strained between them and Oliver? 'Sure,' she said, masking her nerves.

He led her over to the other side of the room. 'Mama, Papa, I'd like to introduce you to Ella O'Brien,' he said.

His voice was much more formal and cool than it had been when he'd introduced her to his brother and sister-in-law, and Ella's heart sank. This didn't bode well.

'Ella, this is my father Edward, the Earl of Darrington, and my mother Catherine, the Countess of Darrington,' Oliver continued.

Instead of greeting her warmly, the way Ned and Prue had, the Earl and Countess of Darrington simply stood there, looking very remote. The Earl nodded at her and the Countess just looked her up and down.

Were they expecting her to curtsey? Did you curtsey to an earl and a countess? Unnerved and flustered, Ella did exactly that. 'Pleased to meet you, Lord and Lady Darrington,' she said awkwardly, hoping she'd got it right.

'Indeed,' the Earl of Darrington said, his voice cool.

Ella noticed that he didn't invite her to use their given names, the way Prue and Ned had done; his approach was much more formal. And she felt as if she'd already made a fool of herself. Perhaps curtseying had been the wrong thing to do.

'So how do you know Oliver?' the Earl asked.

'I'm a midwife. We work together at Teddy's,' she said, acutely aware of the difference between her soft Irish accent and the Earl's cut-glass tones.

'Of course. What do your parents do?' the Countess asked.

'Mama, that's hardly—' Oliver began.

'It's fine,' Ella said. Of course they'd want to know that. 'Mam's a music teacher and Da's a farmer.'

'So you have land in Ireland?' the Countess asked.

'No. Da's a tenant farmer,' Ella said, lifting her chin that little bit higher. She wasn't in the slightest bit ashamed of her background. As far as she was concerned, it didn't matter what your parents did or how much land or money they had—it was who you were as a person and how you treated other people that counted.

And she could understand now why Oliver had a tricky relationship with his parents, and not just because they hadn't wanted him to be a doctor; she knew he thought the same way that she did about people. From his expression, she could tell that he was horrified and angry about the way his parents had reacted to her.

'Ella's a very talented midwife,' Oliver said, his voice very clipped. 'Everyone thinks very highly of her at Teddy's.'

'Indeed,' the Earl drawled. Making it very clear that whatever anyone else thought of her, the Earl and Countess of Darrington didn't think that the daughter of a tenant farmer and a teacher was anywhere near good enough for their son.

'I'm afraid we really ought to mingle. We have rather a lot of guests we haven't welcomed yet,' the Earl said. 'Excuse us, my dear.'

And he and the Countess walked away without even a backward glance.

'I'm so sorry about that,' Oliver said, grimacing.

She swallowed hard. 'It's OK.' Even though it

wasn't. Oliver's parents had just snubbed her. Big time. 'I kind of expected it.'

'My parents,' he said, 'aren't the easiest of people. It really isn't you. That was just plain *rude* of them. Maybe it's because they're stressed about holding a big party.'

Ella didn't think that something as simple as a party would stress the Earl and Countess of Darrington, especially one that had clearly been held every year for a very long time. They would simply snap their fingers and expect things to be done as they ordered. What could there be to worry about? Oliver was just making excuses for them.

Then again, what else could the poor man do?

She was just glad that her own family would be much, much nicer towards Oliver than his parents had been towards her.

Oliver raked a hand through his hair. 'Come on. I'll introduce you to a few others.'

Most of the people at the party seemed to be the movers and shakers of local businesses, plus local landed gentry: the kind of people Ella didn't usually mix with and had nothing in common with. Everyone seemed polite—at least, they weren't as openly hostile towards her as the Earl and Countess had been, but they were still quite reserved with her. It was very obvious that Ella wasn't going to fit into Oliver's world, even though his brother and sister-in-law were nice.

And why did all the men have to wear what smelled like half a bottle of super-strong aftershave? It made her feel queasy again, so she went to splash her face with water.

When she came out of the bathroom, the Countess was waiting outside.

'Feeling a little under the weather?' the Countess enquired, her expression unreadable.

Perhaps Oliver's mother thought she'd been downing too much champagne. Which couldn't have been further from the truth—but the truth was something Ella knew Oliver didn't want the Countess to know yet. 'It's been a busy day,' Ella prevaricated.

'Perhaps I should offer you some coffee.'

Even the thought of it made Ella gag, and she wasn't quite quick enough to hide the reflex.

'I thought as much,' the Countess said. 'I knew there was a reason why Oliver would want to bring someone, especially as it's been a few years since he's turned up to our pre-Christmas drinks party. How far gone are you?'

Faced with a direct question, Ella couldn't lie. 'It's still early days.'

'Hmm. Obviously Oliver will insist on a paternity test, to make *quite* sure. Both he and Ned have known their fair share of women who, let's say, would like to take advantage of their positions.'

What? Oliver's mother actually thought that Ella was lying about Oliver being the baby's father, and that she was some sort of gold-digger—because her parents were ordinary rather than titled? That was outrageous! But Ella couldn't let rip and give the Countess a piece of her mind. She could hardly make a scene in front of everyone at the party, because it would embarrass Oliver hugely.

So she was just going to have to put up with this. And she really hoped that Oliver would think that she'd been gone a little too long and come in search of her, then rescue her from his mother.

'Of course, if it *is* his,' the Countess continued, 'then as a Darrington the baby will have a position to maintain. If it's a boy, he'll go to the same prep school and public school as Edward and Oliver.'

Over my dead body, Ella thought. No way was she dumping her baby in a boarding school. She wanted her child to go to the local school, where he or she would fit in to a normal world. And her child would most definitely grow up feeling loved and wanted, rather than being palmed off on a nanny.

'And,' the Countess said, 'in that case Oliver will have custody of the child.'

What? The baby was so tiny right now that you couldn't make out more than a bean-shape on an ultrasound scan, and the Countess was already planning to take the baby away from her?

Ella opened her mouth, about to say, 'Absolutely *not*,' when the Countess cut in.

'I'm glad we had this little chat, Miss O'Brien. I think we understand each other now.'

The Countess didn't understand her at all, Ella thought, and clearly didn't want to.

'I'll leave you to think about it,' the Countess finished, and swept off.

That told Ella everything she needed to know.

Even though Prue and Ned had been so nice, there was no way she'd ever fit in here. The last thing she wanted was to deepen the divide between Oliver and his parents. So, even though she was angry on his behalf, she wouldn't tell him what his mother had said and risk things getting even worse. Right now the best thing she could do would be to cool things between them instead of letting herself dream that she and Oliver could possibly have a future. It wasn't going to happen.

But this baby was hers and no way was she going to let Oliver's mother take the baby away from her, whatever the Countess might think. If the Countess tried, then she'd have a real fight on her hands. One which Ella had no intention of losing.

Ella had been gone a little too long for Oliver's liking. Had she got lost in the house? Or had something happened? Worried, he excused himself from the people he was talking to and went in search of her.

He found her in a corridor on the way back from the bathroom.

'Are you all right?' he asked.

'Fine,' she said.

She didn't look fine to him. She looked upset. 'Has something happened?'

'No—I'm just a bit tired,' she said.

The baby. Of course. He should've realised. And she'd already excused herself a couple of times to splash water on her face. Clearly something was triggering her morning sickness again. The lilies, maybe? She'd mentioned them earlier.

'Do you want to go?' he asked.

'It's fine,' she said. 'I'm happy to wait until you're ready.'

'I'm ready,' he said. Although it had been good to see Ned again, Oliver was seriously upset by the way his parents had been so cool to Ella, dismissing her. Maybe they were worried he was going to get hurt again, the way he had with Justine—but, as they'd been the ones to introduce him to Justine in the first place and had put so much pressure on them to get together, they were hardly in a position to judge Ella. And he was still furious about the way his mother had grilled Ella about her background. As if it mattered in the slightest what her parents did.

'I really ought to find your parents and thank them for inviting me,' she said.

Oliver would rather leave right now, but he knew Ella was right. Manners were important. It was a pity that his parents seemed to have forgotten that tonight. Though he'd make that point to them later, when Ella wasn't around to be embarrassed by his bluntness.

Thankfully they managed to keep their leave-taking really brief. But Ella was quiet all the way back to Cheltenham. And, when he parked outside her flat, she didn't invite him in for coffee.

Maybe she was tired. It was common for women to be really, really tired in early pregnancy, he reminded himself.

Yet he couldn't shake the feeling that something was wrong. Before the party, he'd kissed her—and she'd definitely responded. Kissed him back. They'd been very close to him picking her up and carrying her to her bed. And the way she'd been so firmly on his side about his career, making him feel that they were in an equal partnership and she'd fight his corner just as hard as he'd fight hers... He'd felt that they'd moved closer, were nearer to understanding each other better and getting to the point where they could agree to make a go of things. And now he realised he knew what he wanted: to be part of her life as well as the baby's. To make a proper family with her.

Right now she'd become remote again. This felt like one step forward and two steps back. Was it because his parents had been so awful? Did she really hate the world he came from? He knew if he asked her what was wrong, she'd say everything was fine. If he tried to kiss her, he had a feeling that this time she wouldn't respond—that he'd be deepening the chasm between them.

How could he get her to talk to him without making things worse?

'Thank you for this evening,' she said politely. 'I'll see you on the ward.'

Maybe the best thing to do now would be to give her some space. 'Sure,' he said, and waited until she was safely indoors before he drove back to his own place.

Was he overreacting, or was Ella going cool on him?

No. He was being ridiculous and paranoid. She'd told him she was tired. And Ella was straightforward. He was just seeing things completely out of context, because seeing his parents always rubbed him up the wrong way. He'd hoped that tonight he could re-establish a better relationship with his parents, or at least the beginnings of one. But they hadn't changed. Right now, he was just out of sorts and seeing shadows where there weren't any. Tomorrow, he'd see Ella on the ward and she'd be her usual sunny self, and everything would be just fine.

It *would*.

CHAPTER SEVEN

ELLA SLEPT BADLY that night. She kept waking up, shivering, after horrible dreams of Oliver delivering the baby and then his mother snatching the child before he could give it to Ella and slamming the door behind her.

When her alarm clanged, Ella was feeling out of sorts and upset. A shower and washing her hair didn't make her feel much better, and she could barely face a single slice of dry toast for breakfast.

She drove in to work and was relieved to discover that Oliver was in a meeting, so she wouldn't have to face him. Even though part of her wanted to tell him about what his mother had said—and to get a bit of reassurance about her nightmare—she knew that wouldn't be fair to him. It'd be like asking him to choose between her and his family. Annabelle was off duty, so

KATE HARDY   197

Ella couldn't discuss it with her, either. Annabelle had texted her that morning.

How did it go?

Ella had texted back with a total fib, saying it
was all fine. She didn't want to burden her best
friend, especially as she knew how hard things
had been for Annabelle and Max. She was glad
it had worked out for them, but at the same time
she felt slightly wistful, as she couldn't see how
things could ever work out between herself and
Oliver. Prue and Ned had been kind, but his parents would never accept her, and Ella didn't want
to be responsible for the final rift between Oliver
and his parents.

'Hey, sweetie. Are you doing OK?'

Ella looked up to see their heavily pregnant
neonatal cardiothoracic surgeon, standing before
her. 'Morning, Sienna. Of course I'm OK. Why
wouldn't I...?' Her voice tailed off as she realised
what Sienna meant. 'Oh. You know.'

''Fraid so.' Sienna patted her arm. 'You've re-
placed me as the hottest topic of gossip at the
Royal Cheltenham, right now.'

Ella bit her lip. 'Hopefully everyone will find something else to think about soon.'

'Of course they will. How did the scan go?'

'Good, thanks. Everything's positive.'

'That's great.' Sienna smiled at her. 'I'm glad that Oliver supported you, too.'

Oh, help. They'd used the cover story that her family was far away so Oliver was supporting her, but had everyone guessed the truth—that Oliver had been there as the baby's father? 'He's the Assistant Head of Obstetrics, so I guess he feels responsible for his staff,' Ella said hesitantly.

'He's a good man. He offered to go with me for my scans, too.'

So Sienna *didn't* know that Oliver was the father of Ella's baby. Which meant that nobody else did either—because Ella knew that Annabelle would've kept her confidence. 'Thanks for not asking.'

'About who the dad is?' Sienna laughed. 'Given my situation, I could hardly be that hypocritical. Sometimes this is just how things happen—and it's much better for a baby to have one parent who really loves them, than two who fight all the time.'

That sounded personal, but Ella wasn't going to intrude by asking. 'Yes, you're right.'

'I just wanted to say, if you need a confidential ear at any time, you know where I am—I know I'm going on leave soon, but I'll still be around.'

'Thanks, Sienna.' It was kind of her to offer, even though Ella thought that the doctor was going to be way too busy with her newborn baby. 'And I'm still on your babysitter list—the bump won't change that.'

'Glad to hear it.' Sienna patted her arm again. 'It'll be good practice for you. We're both used to newborns, but we're also used to handing the babies over and I think it's going to be a bit of a shock to our systems.'

'Ah, but I get to teach new mums how to change nappies and put on a sleep suit,' Ella pointed out.

'Then you have the advantage over me. I know who to call when I get stuck, then.' Sienna smiled. 'Right, I'm due in Theatre. I just wanted to catch you first and see how you were getting on.'

Tears pricked Ella's eyelids. 'That's so kind.'

'And invest in tissues,' Sienna advised. 'You wouldn't believe the stupid things that are going to make you cry. Or how often.'

'I believe you—especially now, because you were right about tins smelling, too,' Ella admitted wryly.

'It'll be fine,' Sienna reassured her. 'See you later.'

'Ella, could we have a wo—?' Oliver began.

She lifted her hands as if shoving him away. 'Sorry—I've been called down to Ultrasound.'

He couldn't argue with that.

But the next time he saw her in a corridor, Ella couldn't stop to have a quick word because she was in a rush on the way to help Jennie, their trainee midwife.

Was he being paranoid, or was she avoiding him?

And she'd been so quiet on the way back to Cheltenham last night.

He'd shared a part of his life with her that he'd always kept private; but, instead of bringing her closer to him, it seemed to have driven her further away.

The third time Oliver tried to talk to Ella, she was backing away as soon as he started speaking.

'Sorry, Oliver. I can't talk right now. I've been called to the Emergency Department.'

'If that was to see the mum with the suspected placental abruption,' he said grimly, 'then you're working with me.'

She bit her lip. 'Oh. I thought I'd be working with Charlie.'

So yet again she'd been hoping to avoid him. 'No. He's in the middle of a complicated delivery.' Hurt made him snap at her. 'So you'll just have to put up with it being me, won't you?'

She gave him a speaking look, but said nothing.

Oliver sighed inwardly. He hated to think that their working relationship was as bad as their personal relationship right now. He knew he should apologise for being abrupt with her, but her coolness had really got to him.

'Ella,' he said when they got into the lift. 'Are you going to be OK with this?'

'An abruption? I've come across them before,' she said coolly.

Oh, great. She'd misunderstood and was about to go prickly on him. 'I don't mean clinically. I know you know your stuff,' he said. 'I meant emotionally. You're pregnant and this might not have a good outcome. If you'd rather someone else took this case, I'll organise that for you.'

'No, it's fine.' She took his hand and squeezed it briefly. 'But thank you for thinking about that.'

Her touch flustered him so much that he didn't say a word until they were in the Emergency Department with Mike Wetherby.

'Courtney Saunders, age thirty-six, and she's currently thirty-four weeks,' Mike explained. 'This is her second baby; her last pregnancy and birth were straightforward, and this pregnancy's been straightforward so far but today she slipped on the ice while she was getting off the bus and had quite a bad fall. She tried to protect the baby by throwing herself sideways; she banged her hip and her head. I've sorted that side of it out for her, and obviously there's still a bit of tachycardia but I think that's probably stress.'

Though it could also be a precursor to other complications, Oliver knew. 'How's the baby doing?'

'That's why I called you,' Mike said. 'She says she hasn't felt the baby move much since the fall, her back hurts, and she thinks she's having Braxton Hicks.'

'But you don't think it's Braxton Hicks?' Oliver asked.

'I have a bad feeling about this,' Mike said. 'She doesn't have any signs of bleeding but, given the fall and the length of her pregnancy, I think it might be a concealed abruption. That's why I called you guys rather than doing a manual exam myself.'

'Good call,' Oliver said. If it was an abruption, a manual exam would make things much worse. 'Have you managed to contact her partner or a friend to be with her?'

'We tried her partner, but he's in a meeting, so we've left a message for him either to call us or to come straight in,' Mike said. 'I'll introduce you to Courtney.'

Once Mike had introduced Oliver and Ella and headed off to treat his next patient, Oliver said, 'Mrs Saunders—may I call you Courtney?' At her nod, he continued, 'I'd like to examine you, if I may.'

Courtney gave her consent, and Oliver examined her gently. 'Tell me if there's any pain or tenderness,' he said.

'I'm fine. I can put up with being a bit sore

and the Braxton Hicks. But I'm scared about the baby,' she said.

Ella took her hand to reassure her. 'That's why we're here. Oliver's the Assistant Head of Obstetrics, so he's really good at his job.'

'Assistant Head of Obstetrics?' Courtney looked panicky. 'Does that mean it's really serious?'

'It simply means,' Oliver said gently, 'that all my other obstetricians are in Theatre or in clinics right now and I happened to be the doctor who was free. It's nothing sinister, I promise. But what I'm going to do first is reassure you by checking the baby, OK? Once I've listened to the heartbeat, Ella's going to put some wires on you so we can monitor how the baby's doing and keep an eye on—do you know if it's a boy or a girl?'

Courtney shook her head. 'We didn't want to know. But Alex—he's my oldest—he tells everyone he's going to have a little sister.'

'Baby Saunders, then,' Oliver said with a smile. 'And we'll also measure how your contractions are doing.' He took the Pinard stethoscope and listened to the baby's heartbeat, then smiled at Courtney. 'That's a nice strong heartbeat, so that's good news.' It was a little slow for his liking, but he wasn't going to worry Courtney about that just now. Not until he'd checked the ultrasound. 'Before Ella puts the wires on, I'd also like to give you an ultrasound scan—it's just like the ones you've had before, when you came in at twenty weeks.'

And the scan showed him the one thing he'd hoped it wouldn't. He glanced across at Ella who mouthed, 'Abruption?' At his tiny nod, she mouthed, 'Line in and cross-match?'

He was glad she was so quick to pick things up—and he was even more glad that she was professional enough not to let the difficulties between them affect their patient.

He turned the screen so that Courtney could see it. 'When you fell, Courtney, it caused part of the placenta to start to come away from the wall of your womb—this dark area here shows bleeding behind the womb, which is why you're not seeing any spotting,' he said. 'It's what we call a placental abruption.'

Courtney turned pale. 'Can you stitch it back or something?'

'Unfortunately we can't reattach the placenta,'

he said. 'If a mum has a small tear in the placenta and the baby's doing OK, we can send her home to wait it out, or we can admit her to Teddy's and see how things go—but this is quite a big tear. It means that right now your baby isn't getting enough oxygen and nutrients from the placenta, and the baby's heartbeat is getting slower.'

'Is my baby going to die?' Courtney asked, her eyes wide with panic.

'We're going to do our best to keep your baby safe,' Ella said.

'And the safest thing for me to do is to deliver the baby now through an emergency Caesarean section,' Oliver finished.

'But it's too early for me to have the baby!' Courtney said. 'I'm only thirty-four weeks— there's another six weeks to go yet.'

'The baby's going to be small,' Oliver said, 'but I promise you at thirty-four weeks Baby Saunders will manage just fine. I'm going to give you steroids to help mature the baby's lungs.'

'Like bodybuilders use?' Courtney asked.

'No, they're corticosteroids, like the ones the body produces naturally or people with asthma take to help with their airways,' Ella explained.

'Babies born before thirty-seven weeks sometimes have trouble breathing because their lungs aren't developed fully. The steroids help the lungs develop so the baby doesn't have breathing problems.'

Oliver didn't chip in; he was enjoying watching Ella in action. She was so good with patients, explaining things simply in terms they could understand.

She'd be a good mum, too, he thought wistfully. But would she give him the chance to be a good dad?

He shook himself. Now wasn't the time. Their patient had to come first. But he'd try to find a good time for him and Ella to talk. They really, really needed to talk about the baby—and about them.

'What happens is we give you an injection,' Ella continued, 'and the steroids go through your bloodstream and through the placenta into the baby's body and lungs. And as well as being able to breathe better, the baby can suck better and take in more milk.'

'So the baby won't have side-effects?' Courtney asked.

'No, and neither will you,' Ella reassured her.

'But Ryan isn't here yet. He can't miss our baby being born,' Courtney said, a tear running down her cheek.

'I'll try him again,' Ella said, and squeezed her hand. 'I'm just going to put a butterfly in the back of your hand so we can give you any drugs we need, and then I'll call him myself—Mike said he was in a meeting so they left a message, but I'll make sure I actually speak to him.' She smiled at Courtney. 'I know this is really scary, but you're in the best place.'

Once Ella had put the line in, cross-matched Courtney's blood and set up continuous foetal monitoring for the baby's heartbeat and Courtney's contractions, she went off to call Courtney's partner.

'I can't believe this is happening. I wish I'd stopped work last week instead of trying to keep going a bit longer,' Courtney said.

'Hey, it could've happened anyway,' Oliver said. 'You might have slipped on your front doorstep, or when you were taking Alex out to the park.' He sat next to her and held her hand. 'There is something else I need to talk to you about, Courtney. With an abruption like this, it's possible that you might lose a lot of blood—we can't tell from the scan how much blood you've already lost. That's why Ella cross-matched you, so we can make sure we can sort that out and give you more blood if you need it. But if I can't stop the bleeding once I've delivered the baby, I might have to give you a hysterectomy.'

Courtney looked dismayed. 'You mean—like someone who's near the menopause?'

'Sort of,' Oliver said. 'I know you're very young and you might want to have more children, so I'm hoping it'll all be straightforward. But I do need to prepare you for the worst-case scenario too—because if that happens then a hysterectomy might be the only way I can save your life.'

'So this abruption thing could kill me as well as the baby?'

'That's the very worst-case scenario,' Oliver stressed. 'In most cases it's fine. But I do need you to sign a consent form just in case the very worst happens.'

'I…' Courtney shook her head, looking dazed. 'It's a lot to take in. This morning I was planning to work for another month, and now I've fallen when I got off the bus I might die and so might the baby.'

'Very, very worst-case,' Oliver said. 'But that's why I want to deliver the baby now, to give him or her the best possible chance.'

'There isn't really a choice, is there?' she asked miserably. 'All right. I'll sign your form.'

By the time she'd signed the form and Oliver had administered the steroids, Ella came back into the room, smiling. 'I've spoken to Ryan. He's on his way now and he says to tell you he loves you and everything's going to be all right.'

A tear trickled down Courtney's face. 'Even though I nearly killed our baby?'

'You did nothing of the sort. It was an accident,' Ella reassured her. 'And your man will be here really soon. He says to tell you he's going to make the world speed record for getting across town.'

Courtney's lower lip wobbled, but she tried her best to smile.

'So what happens now is the anaesthetist is on her way. She's going to give you an anaesthetic, and then Oliver will make an incision here—' she sketched the shape on Courtney's tummy '—so he can deliver the baby.'

'Can Ryan be there?' Courtney asked.

'If he does that world speed record,' Ella said with a smile, 'then he can be there and he can cut the cord. I'll be there, too, to look after Baby Saunders. Once I've checked the baby over, you can both get to see him or her and have a cuddle.'

'What if—if it's the worst-case scenario?' Courtney asked, a catch in her voice.

'Then I'll take Ryan off to one side with the baby so Oliver can sort everything out. But he's the best surgeon I know. You're in good hands.'

If only she had as much confidence in him personally as she had in him professionally, Oliver thought. Though part of it was his own fault. He'd held back from her. If he told her about Justine, then maybe she'd understand why he was having a hard time getting his head round the fact that he was going to be a dad—and why he needed to feel that he was in control of everything. But then again, letting her close enough to meet his family had backfired.

This whole thing was a mess.

But doing the job he did, seeing how important family was to the women he helped to give birth and their partners... It was beginning to make him realise that he wanted this, too. He didn't want to be just a dad. He wanted to be a partner, too. He wanted to be loved for who he was.

But what did Ella want? Could they make a go of things together? Could they become a family, the kind of family that he hadn't grown up in but suspected that she had?

By the time the anaesthetist had administered the spinal block, Ryan had arrived for a tearful reunion with his wife. Oliver glanced at Ella and saw the wistfulness on her face. So was this affecting her, too?

Their talk would have to wait until after this operation. But Oliver was determined to sit down and talk to Ella properly and find out what she wanted—and, with any luck, it would be the same thing that he wanted. And then they could move forward properly. Together.

Thankfully, delivering the baby and the placenta stopped the bleeding, so he didn't have to give Courtney a hysterectomy. And their little girl, although tiny and in need of a day or two in the neonatal unit, looked as if she was going to do very well indeed.

Once he'd finished the operation and Courtney

had gone through to the recovery room, he was on his own with Ella.

'Can we take ten minutes?' he asked. 'I'll buy you a cup of tea, if you like.'

'Thanks, but I need to be elsewhere,' she said. 'I promised to help Jennie with her studies.'

Again? His heart sank. This sounded like another evasion tactic. Maybe he was wrong about this after all, and she didn't want the same thing that he did. 'Ella, I think we need to talk.'

'No need,' she said with a brisk smile. 'Everything's fine.'

He didn't think so; and, from the expression in her eyes, neither did she.

'How about dinner tonight?'

'Sorry,' she said. 'I really do have to go.'

Which left Oliver to walk back to his office alone.

He sat at his desk, trying to concentrate on his pile of admin, and wondering how everything between him and Ella had gone so wrong. Was it his imagination, or was she finding excuses to be anywhere but near him?

And how was he ever going to persuade her to give him a chance?

He was beginning to think that he needed a Christmas miracle. Except they were in very short supply, and in any case he ought to be able to sort this out on his own.

CHAPTER EIGHT

'YOU LOOK TERRIBLE, ELLA,' Annabelle informed her best friend. 'Rough night?'

'I'm fine,' Ella fibbed.

'I've known you for a lot of years now,' Annabelle said softly, 'and you're not fine. What's wrong?'

Ella grimaced. It was all so complicated. Where did she even start?

'That was a pretty stupid question,' Annabelle said. 'Obviously it's Oliver.'

'Not so much Oliver as his family,' Ella admitted.

Annabelle winced. 'I thought you said Thursday night went OK?'

'Bits of it did,' Ella said. 'His brother's nice, and so is his sister-in-law.'

'So the problem's his parents?'

Ella nodded miserably. But she couldn't tell Annabelle the whole story. It wasn't hers to tell, and it wouldn't be fair to break Oliver's confidence; Ella was the only person in the department who knew about his background. But she could tell Annabelle some of it, and maybe Annabelle would have some ideas about how to deal with it. 'His mum wants me to have a paternity test.'

'What?' Annabelle looked shocked. 'That's ridiculous.'

But it didn't bother Ella anywhere near as much as the other thing that the Countess had suggested. 'And she wants Oliver to have custody of the baby.'

Annabelle frowned. 'What does Oliver say about it?'

'He doesn't know,' Ella admitted. 'He wasn't there when she said it.'

'Then talk to him about it. Tell him what she said.'

'That's the problem. I can't,' Ella said. 'He doesn't get on that well with his parents.'

'Then obviously he'll take your side. And no way is he going to take the baby from you.'

Oh, but he could. Especially if she had a boy and Prue had a girl—because then Ella's baby could be the future Earl of Darrington. But explaining that wouldn't be fair to Oliver. 'It's complicated,' Ella hedged. 'And I don't want to make things worse between Oliver and his parents. It wouldn't be fair to make him choose sides.'

'Talk to him,' Annabelle advised. 'And if Oliver Darrington's even half the man I think he is, he'll tell his mother to back off and to start treating you with a bit of courtesy.'

'I'm not even officially his girlfriend,' Ella pointed out.

'He took you to meet his family. Which he wouldn't have done if he wasn't serious about trying to make a go of things with you,' Annabelle countered.

But Oliver hadn't said anything about his feelings. And Ella didn't want to try to make a go of it just for the sake of the baby. Sienna's words rang all too true: *It's much better for a baby to have one parent who really loves them, than two who fight all the time.*

But, before she and Annabelle could discuss it any more, Jennie rushed over to them. 'Ella, you're needed in Room One,' she said. 'It's Georgina.'

'Georgina? As in Georgie, our mum-to-be with

quads?' Ella asked. Georgina was one of Ella's special patients; after IVF treatment, the two embryos implanted had each split into identical twins, so Georgina was expecting quadruplets. 'But she's not due in for another appointment until next week.'

'She thinks she's in labour,' Jennie said.

It was way too early for Georgina to be in labour. 'I'm coming now,' Ella said. She squeezed Annabelle's hand. 'Thanks for letting me talk. I'll catch up with you later.'

'Sure. Call me if you need anything.'

'I will,' Ella promised.

She went into Room One, where Georgina was sitting on the bed, looking worried. The younger woman's face brightened when she saw Ella.

'How are you doing, Georgie?' Ella asked.

'A bit scared. I think I'm in labour,' Georgina said.

'Is Leo not with you?' Georgina's partner had been to every single appointment with her.

'He's in New York. I called him and he's getting the first plane back.' Georgina bit her lip. 'Mum's got the vomiting bug that's going round, and she doesn't want to give it to me, or she'd be here to hold my hand—but she's texted me a dozen times since I told her I was coming in.'

But texting wasn't the same as having someone with you, especially if you were scared, Ella knew. 'OK. Let's have a look at what your lovely babies are up to,' Ella said with a smile. 'Jennie, can you see if Charlie's around, please? He'll want to see his patient immediately. And can you get the portable scanner, please?'

'Sure,' the trainee midwife said.

'So are you having contractions, Georgie?' Ella asked. 'And have you timed them?'

'I'm not sure—I think I'm getting twinges or something, but it doesn't hurt as much as I expected and they're all over the place. But, Ella, my tummy feels *weird*,' Georgina said. 'It's all tight and shiny. My back aches. And I feel as if I've put on half a stone overnight.'

Alarm bells rang in the back of Ella's head. She didn't want to worry Georgina, but this didn't sound like the beginnings of labour. It sounded like a complication—and, given that Georgina was carrying four babies, this could be a very tricky complication. 'Would you mind baring your tummy for me so I can have a look?' she asked, keeping her voice light and cheery.

'Of course,' Georgina said, and pulled up her top while she leaned back against the pillows.

Georgina's abdomen definitely looked tight and shiny, as she'd said. But Ella wasn't sure this was labour. She had a nasty feeling that one of the quads might be in trouble.

'As soon as Charlie gets here,' Ella said, 'we'll have a look on the ultrasound and see if they're all waving at you this time.'

Georgina smiled, but Ella could tell that the young mum-to-be was panicking.

'I'll take your blood pressure while we're waiting for Charlie,' she said.

At least Georgina's blood pressure was normal, but Ella would be a lot happier once she'd monitored all the babies.

Just then, Oliver walked in with Jennie, pushing the portable scanner. Ella's heart skipped a beat when she saw him.

'Sorry, Charlie's in Theatre. Will I do?' he asked.

Provided they could keep their private life out of it, yes. 'Georgie, this is Oliver Darrington, our

KATE HARDY   221

Assistant Head of Obstetrics,' Ella said. 'Oliver, this is Georgie. She's twenty-eight weeks and she's expecting quads.'

'Congratulations,' Oliver said, smiling at her.

'Thank you,' Georgina said.

'Georgie thinks she might be in labour,' Ella said. 'Her blood pressure's fine, but we need to do a scan to see what the babies are up to.'

'OK. I'm sorry, Georgie, our gel's a bit cold,' Oliver apologised. 'May I?'

'Sure.'

Once the scan of the babies was on the screen, Ella spotted the problem immediately. The two girl quads were fine, but the two boys were definitely struggling; one of them had a lot of amniotic fluid in the sac, while the other had very little and was practically stuck against the wall of Georgie's womb. The bigger boy twin had a full bladder; Ella couldn't see the smaller twin's bladder, but if her suspicions were right it wasn't full.

'Oliver, can we have a quick word?' she asked, not wanting to worry Georgina by discussing her fears in front of her.

'Sure. Would you excuse us a moment, Georgie?' Oliver asked with a smile.

Georgie nodded.

'Jennie, perhaps you can get Georgie a drink and make her comfortable for the next couple of minutes?' Ella asked.

'Thanks,' Georgina said. 'I have been feeling a bit thirsty, the last day or two.'

It was another maternal sign for twin-to-twin transfusion, Ella knew, and her misgivings increased. She waited until they were outside the room and the door was closed before she turned to Oliver. 'I've been Georgie's named midwife since day one and Charlie's her named doctor—the quads have all been doing just fine, and Georgie was only in for a scan last week,' Ella said. 'When she told me her symptoms this morning and I examined her, I wondered if it might be twin-to-twin transfusion.'

'Good call. The scan pretty much proved that,' Oliver said.

'But how could it happen so fast? Everything was fine last week. I've kept a really close eye on her because obviously with carrying quads she's a high-risk mum.'

'She's in her last trimester,' Oliver said, 'so it's an acute form of the condition rather than a chronic one—and acute TTT can happen practically overnight.'

'So what are the options?' Ella asked. 'I've seen less than half a dozen cases of TTT in my career. Do we deliver the babies early, or do you put a hole in the membrane between the twins, or could you do laser surgery on the placenta to separate their bloodstreams?'

'It's a difficult call,' Oliver said. 'If you put a hole in the membrane so the twins share one sac, there's a risk of entangling the umbilical cords, and that's something I'd rather do at an earlier stage than Georgina's at. This has all happened really quickly, so there's a possibility that the recipient quad has a heart problem, because the excess blood and fluid will have put strain on his heart.' He frowned. 'I'd like to call Juliet Turner in.'

'Juliet Turner?' Ella asked.

'She's a neonatal specialist surgeon and she's got a fabulous reputation for her work in utero. She might be able to operate on the quads if need be.'

'What aren't you telling me?'

'She's in Australia,' Oliver admitted.

'So it'll be at least a day before she can get here—*if* she agrees to come,' Ella pointed out. 'And you're just expecting the poor woman to drop everything and travel halfway round the world to come and treat Georgie's babies?'

'Juliet's a professional.'

'Surely there's someone closer than Australia?' Ella asked.

'Juliet's the best,' Oliver said simply, 'which is the whole point of Teddy's. We can keep Georgina and the babies comfortable until she gets here.'

Ella was about to say that Juliet Turner might already have commitments which prevented her from rushing all the way from Australia to Cheltenham, but Oliver had the kind of stubborn expression that told her he'd talk the surgeon into changing any commitments for the sake of Georgina and the quads.

'OK,' she said. 'And I guess that gives Leo— the quads' dad—a chance to get here from New York. Let's tell her together.'

She went back in with Oliver and sat on the bed, taking Georgina's hand.

'Everything's not all right, is it?' Georgina asked. 'What's happening to my babies?'

'It's something called twin-to-twin transfusion,' Ella explained. 'You know you've got two sets of identical twins.'

'Two boys and two girls—Graham, Rupert, Lily and Rose,' Georgina said.

'Lovely names,' Oliver said. 'Two of my nieces are called Lily and Rose.'

'What's wrong with them?' Georgina asked.

'Lily and Rose are both fine,' Ella reassured her. 'But Graham and Rupert have a problem.

Normally identical twins share a placenta, and the blood flows evenly between the babies, so they both get the same amount of blood flow and nutrition. But sometimes there's a problem with the blood vessels so one twin gets too much and one doesn't get enough. The twin that gets too much blood wees more, and that produces more amniotic fluid round him, and the twin that doesn't get enough wees less and has less amniotic fluid. That's why it's called twin-to-twin transfusion.'

'Are they—will they be all right?' Georgina asked. 'And was it something I did?'

'It's definitely not anything you did,' Oliver said. 'It just happens, sometimes.'

'You did the best thing by coming straight in to us when you weren't feeling right,' Ella added.

'And we'll do our very best to keep them healthy,' Oliver said. 'There are several things we can do, but I'd like to bring in a specialist who's very, very experienced at doing surgery in the womb.'

'You're going to operate on one of the boys while they're still inside me?' Georgina asked, looking shocked.

'That depends on what Juliet thinks is the best thing to do,' Oliver said, 'but it's a possibility. You can discuss your options with Dr Warren, too. I know he's been your named doctor since day one, so it's important that you talk to him.'

'So when's this going to happen?' Georgina asked. 'Today? Because I want Leo here.'

'Ella told me he's coming from New York. Don't worry, it won't be today,' Oliver said, 'so there's plenty of time for him to get here.'

'We're going to keep you in for a few days,' Ella said. 'I want to monitor the babies, so we'll be hooking you up with some wires, and we'll keep you comfortable until Juliet gets here.'

'Can't Charlie do the operation?' Georgina asked.

'Juliet has much more experience,' Oliver said. 'And I'm sure Charlie will be in to see you as soon as he's out of Theatre and he will explain everything. I'm due in clinic, but if you need me then Ella will give me a call.'

'Thank you,' Georgina said.

Charlie came in as soon as he was out of Theatre. 'I'm so sorry I wasn't here, Georgie.' Standing by the bed, he quickly read her case notes. He had been informed there was a situation on the way from Theatre. 'Ella, who diagnosed the TTT?'

Ella filled him in on everything except Juliet's potential involvement; it wasn't her place to tell Charlie.

'I understand it's a little overwhelming, Georgie,' Charlie said. 'But there are treatment options. Don't think the worst. We might not have to deliver the babies early.'

'Oliver said the babies might have an operation in my womb,' Georgina said.

'It's a possibility, but we'll discuss every option

with you and Leo and we'll go ahead the way you want us to go,' Charlie reassured her.

Ella stayed with Georgina until the end of her shift; but then she discovered that Lexie, the midwife who was meant to take over from her for the night shift, had gone down with the vomiting bug.

'Don't worry. I'll stay with you, Georgie,' Ella promised.

'But—you've been working all day.'

'That's fine,' Ella said with a smile. 'You're one of my mums, and I'm not leaving you while you're worried.'

Clearly Oliver wasn't happy about the situation when he heard about it, because he came to the door of Georgina's room. 'A word, Ella?'

'How did you get on with Juliet?' she asked, hoping to head him off.

'She'll be here on Monday. But that wasn't what I wanted to talk to you about.' He sighed. 'Ella, you can't work a double shift.'

Ordering her about *again*. 'Watch me,' Ella said grimly. 'You know the situation. Lexie's gone down with the virus.'

'Health and Safety would have the biggest hissy fit in the world.'

Ella shrugged. 'Their problem. I'm not leaving Georgie.'

'I can get an agency nurse in to cover Lexie's shift. Ella, you need to look after yourself.' His face tightened. 'And our baby.'

'Georgie's worried as it is,' Ella pointed out. 'I'm not leaving her to be looked after by someone she's never met before. She knows me and she's comfortable with me.'

'And you're putting your health at risk.'

'OK, then. I'm off duty—and I'm visiting someone in Teddy's.'

'Now you're being ridiculous.' Oliver scowled at her.

'I'm not. I care about my mums, and I'm not deserting someone who right now is on her own and worried sick about her babies. Georgie's mum has the vomiting bug, so she can't come in, and her husband's on a plane back from New York. That means that Georgie's on her own, knowing there's something wrong with one of her babies and worrying that the worst is going to happen. I'm not just walking out of that door and leaving her to it.'

* * *

Oliver sighed. Why did Ella feel that she had to prove herself over and over again? 'You're a good midwife, Ella. Everyone in Teddy's knows that.'

She lifted her chin. 'Thank you.'

'But you also have to remember that you're pregnant. You can't work a twenty-four-hour shift. I wouldn't let a non-pregnant member of staff do that, let alone one who's pregnant.'

Ella shrugged. 'Then I'm a visitor who's staying.'

A stubborn visitor. 'Just promise me you'll put your feet up, you won't rush around, and you'll eat properly.'

'I'm not stupid, Oliver.'

'I know that.'

'I'm not going to do anything reckless or anything that could hurt the baby. But I can't just walk away and leave Georgie worrying. Can't you see that?'

Yes, he could. Because Ella was sweet and kind and was always the first to offer help. 'All right,' he said. 'You can stay with her as a visitor, provided you put your feet up and rest properly. But you are absolutely *not* working. I'll get agency cover.'

'As long as the agency midwife knows that I'm Georgie's named midwife and to run everything past me,' Ella insisted.

If he didn't agree, he knew Ella would find a way of breaking the rules and work a double shift. 'All right,' he said.

But two could play that game. And he made quite sure that Ella had a proper evening meal, because he brought it in to her himself on a tray. 'No arguments,' he said.

And he could see in her expression that she knew he'd call her on the situation in front of Georgie if she refused the meal—and he'd stay until she'd eaten it, if he had to. 'Thank you,' she said. 'That's really kind of you and it looks scrumptious.'

When Oliver had left the room and closed the door behind him, Georgie asked, 'What's with the special treatment? Are you two an item?'

Not really, Ella thought. She wished they were, but it wasn't going to happen because his parents would never accept her. So she couldn't answer

Georgie's question honestly. 'Oliver looks after all his team,' she said. Which was true: sometimes she wondered what drove him to be so protective. 'And I'm pregnant.'

'Congratulations,' Georgie asked. 'When's it due? That is, I take it you're having just one and not quads?'

Ella smiled. 'No, just the one baby. It's early days. The baby's so tiny at the moment it looks like a little bean on the scan.' She took her phone from her pocket and flicked through to the photograph she'd taken of the scan picture. 'Look, that's my little one.'

'Your first?'

Ella nodded. 'And that's scary enough. I can't imagine what it's like to be expecting quads.'

'Really scary,' Georgie said. 'I never thought we'd be able to have children at all. It was a miracle that two embryos took—and even more of a miracle that both of them then became twins.'

Her baby was a miracle, too, Ella thought. Not that she wanted to discuss that. 'Two girls and two boys—and they'll all grow up close. That's nice.'

'All the way through, I've been so scared that

we'd lose one of them,' Georgie said. 'All the stories you see on the Internet.'

'Which do nothing but make new mums worry,' Ella said. 'Ignore them.'

'I had—but now with this twin-to-twin thing…'

Ella took her hand. 'Try not to worry. Oliver says Juliet's the best and she'll be able to keep your boys safe.'

'I hope so,' Georgie said.

Oliver came in twice more that evening—the first to check that everything was fine, and the second to bring both Georgie and Ella a mug of hot chocolate.

And then the penny dropped for Ella.

Oliver was officially off duty right now and had been for a while, but he was still here at the hospital. Was he checking up on her? She pushed the thought away. Of course it wasn't that he didn't trust her. She'd made him aware of his bossy tendencies, so it was more likely that he was worried about her but he was trying not to make the sort of fuss that would annoy her.

'Shouldn't you be at home by now?' she asked. She saw the flash of guilt in his eyes, and knew that her guess had been right.

'I'm catching up on some paperwork, so I thought I'd take a break and keep you both company for a bit.'

'Oliver, it's ten o'clock and you're on an early shift tomorrow.'

His expression said very clearly, *Yes, and you've been in all day.*

'Go home,' she said gently, 'and get some sleep.'

'Are you sure you're going to be all right here?'

'I'm sure. And I'm on a late tomorrow, so I'm going to laze around all morning.' She knew he'd pick up what she wasn't saying in front of Georgie: *don't fuss.* Though, at the same time, it warmed her that he was concerned and trying not to be overbearing about it.

If only his family was different...

But that wasn't fair. It wasn't his fault.

'I'll see you later, then,' he said. 'Call me if you need anything.'

'I will,' she promised.

But he came in again on his way out of the department, this time carrying a blanket, which he proceeded to tuck round her. Georgie had fallen asleep, so he simply mouthed, 'Call me,' rested the backs of his fingers briefly against her cheek, and left the room as quietly as he could.

Ella had to blink back the tears. This was the man she'd fallen for—kind, considerate and caring. But his parents would never accept her in his life. She couldn't ask him to choose between them. Somehow, she'd have to find a way of backing off without either of them getting hurt.

Except she had a nasty feeling it was already too late for that.

She dozed in the chair next to Georgie's bed, waking only when the agency midwife came in to check on them, until Leo arrived at the crack of dawn the next morning. Ella talked him through what was happening with the babies, drawing diagrams and labelling them to help him understand.

'Sorry, my writing's terrible,' she said, wincing. At times like this, she really resented her dyslexia.

'It's because you're a medic,' Leo said with a smile. 'All medics have terrible handwriting.'

'I guess,' she said.

She stayed with Georgie and Leo until the midwife from the early shift took over.

'Thank you for staying with me,' Georgie said. 'That was above and beyond the call of duty.'

'Any time,' Ella said, meaning it. 'I'm going home for a nap now, but if you need me just ask one of the midwives to call me, OK?'

'You're the best, Ella,' Leo said, giving her a hug. 'Thank you.'

'No problem. Sit and cuddle your wife,' she said with a smile.

CHAPTER NINE

ELLA'S CAR HAD frozen over during the night. With a sigh, she scraped the ice off the windscreen and climbed into the car. Fortunately she was on a late today so she could go home, have a cup of tea and a bath, then set her alarm and have a sleep before her shift.

As she drove back towards her flat, she noticed a car coming up to the junction of a side road on her left. To her shock, it didn't manage to stop at the junction but slid on the ice and crashed straight into her. The impact pushed her right across the road into a line of parked cars.

She checked to see it was safe to get out of the car, then did so. She could see straight away that her car was undriveable and she'd need to call the insurance company to tow her car away.

The other driver came over to her. 'I'm so sorry, love. The road wasn't gritted and I just couldn't stop,' he said.

'The roads are pretty bad. I guess we'd better swap insurance details,' she said tiredly and reached into the car for her handbag. She took out a pen and notebook, but when she took out her reading glasses she saw that the coloured lenses had cracked during the impact. She didn't have a spare pair with her, so now she was going to make a mess of this and probably get half the numbers in the wrong place.

'Are you all right, love?' the other driver asked, clearly seeing that she was close to tears.

'I'm dyslexic,' she said, gesturing to her ruined glasses, 'and without these I'm going to get everything wrong.'

'Let me do it,' he said. 'It's the least I can do, seeing as it was my fault. You sit down in the warm, love, and I'll sort it out.'

He wrote down all the information for her, called the police to inform them about the accident and her insurance company so they could arrange to pick up her car, and waited with her until the tow truck arrived. Thankfully it turned up only half an hour later, but by then Ella was shivering and desperately tired.

'Are you sure you're all right? You've not

banged your head or anything?' the tow truck driver asked.

'No, just my reading glasses are wrecked,' she said wearily. 'I was lucky. It could've been an awful lot worse.'

'We've had so many cars sliding off the road this morning—the gritters clearly didn't think it was going to freeze this badly last night,' the tow truck driver said. He took her car to the repair garage and then drove her back to her flat. 'I'm only supposed to take you to one or the other,' he said, 'but I remember you. You delivered my youngest last year. My wife had a rough time and you were brilliant with her.'

Ella was really grateful. 'Thank you so much. Do you want a cup of tea or something?'

'That's kind of you, but I'd better not. I've got half a dozen other crashes to go to,' he said wryly. 'Take care.'

Ella let herself into her flat, started running a bath and put the kettle on. Then, when she undressed, she realised there was blood in her knickers.

She was spotting.

Ice slid down her spine. She'd felt a sharp jerk

across her shoulder and abdomen from the seatbelt when the other car had crashed into her, but her car's airbag hadn't gone off and she hadn't banged herself against the steering wheel. She hadn't thought the crash was bad enough to warrant going to hospital; she'd felt OK at the time, there had probably been dozens of other accidents on the icy roads and there were drivers more in need of urgent medical attention than her.

But now she was spotting, at eight weeks of pregnancy, and that wasn't a good thing.

Oh, God. Please don't let her lose the baby. It hadn't been planned, but it was oh, so wanted.

'Hang on in there, little one,' she whispered, with one hand wrapped protectively round her bump.

With shaking hands, she rang Annabelle, but her best friend wasn't answering her home phone or her mobile. Ella was sure that Annabelle was off duty today; but maybe she was out with Max somewhere and her phone was accidentally in silent mode.

Ella didn't want to ring an ambulance, because she knew how busy the hospital was right now, and someone else could need to go to the emergency department more urgently. Maybe she should get a taxi in to the Royal Cheltenham?

But right now she was so scared. She really didn't want to do this on her own.

Oliver.

Given how things were between them and that he'd been so fed up that she'd stayed with Georgina all night after her shift, worrying that she was overdoing things and putting the baby at risk, Oliver was the last person she wanted to call. But her brain was on a go-slow and she couldn't think of anyone else. Plus he was the baby's father—he had the right to know that there was a problem.

It took her three attempts before she managed to call his mobile.

'Darrington,' Oliver said absently, as if he hadn't even looked at the screen.

'It's Ella,' she said.

'Ella? Is everything all right?'

Her teeth had started to chatter and she could hardly get the words out.

'Ella, what's happened?' he asked urgently.

'A c-car crashed into me on the way h-home, and now I'm s-spotting.'

'Are you at home?'

'Y-yes.'

'I'm on my way to you right now,' he said. 'Try not to worry. I'll call you when I'm in the car so you're not going to be on your own while you're waiting, and I'll be with you very, very soon, OK?'

Ella had had a car accident and she was spotting. That wasn't good.

Please, please don't let her lose the baby, Oliver begged inwardly.

The shock of her news had made him realise just how much he wanted the baby.

He headed out to Reception and was really grateful that Annabelle was there; she'd changed duty at the last minute to help cover sick leave.

'Is everything all right?' she asked.

'No. Ella's been in an accident. She just called me and said she's spotting. I'm going to get her now, so please can you make sure the portable scanner's in one of the rooms and keep it free? I'm bringing her straight in to Teddy's.'

'Got you. Give her my love and tell her not to worry,' Annabelle said. 'Drive safely.'

'I will.'

As soon as he was in the car, Oliver switched his phone over to the hands-free system and called Ella as he drove to her flat. He could hear the tears in her voice when she answered; it ripped him apart that she was crying and right now he couldn't comfort her properly or do anything to fix this. But until he'd done the scan and knew what was going on, he couldn't give her the reassurance he really wanted to give her.

'Ella, I'm on my way now,' he said. 'Teddy's is on standby and Annabelle's there—she sends her love.'

'But Annabelle's off duty.'

'No, she swapped duty yesterday to help me out with sick leave cover,' he said.

He heard a sob. 'I'm meant to be on a late today.'

'Don't worry about that right now,' he soothed. 'We can sort it out later.'

'I never meant for this to happen when I stayed with Georgie,' she said. 'I would never, ever put the baby at risk.'

'I know and you did the right thing—the kind thing,' he said. 'You'd have been worrying yourself silly about Georgie and the quads if you'd just gone home.' Because that was who Ella was: dedicated to her job.

'The crash wasn't my fault, Oliver. It really wasn't. The other driver just couldn't stop at the junction and ploughed into me.'

Why did she seem to think he was angry with her? 'Ella, I'm not going to shout at you.'

'You were near shouting at me yesterday.'

She had a point. He'd gone into overprotective mode when she'd suggested working a double shift. 'I'm sorry. I'm a grumpy sod and you have the right to tell me to shut up when I start ranting,' he said.

To his relief, he heard what sounded almost like a wry chuckle. But then there was another muffled sob. 'Hold on, honey. I'm going to be there very soon,' he said. 'And, Ella, I'm glad you called me.'

'Really?' She didn't sound as if she believed him.

'Really,' he said firmly.

He kept her talking all the way from his house to her flat. When he got there, he didn't bother about a parking permit—he'd willingly pay a dozen parking fines if he had to—but just ran over to her door and rang the bell. When she opened her door, he pulled her straight into his arms and held her close. 'Everything's going to be all right, I promise.'

'I don't want to lose the baby.' Her shoulders heaved.

'You're not going to lose the baby, not if I have anything to do with it,' he said. 'Let's go.' He locked the front door behind her, held her close all the way to his car, helped her in and then drove to the Royal Cheltenham, holding her hand between gear changes. She was trembling and he desperately wanted to hold her; but he knew that if he stopped to comfort her it would be that much longer before he could give her a scan and see what was going on. 'We're not going to the Emergency Department. I'll do the scan myself at Teddy's so you don't have to wait.'

'I'm so scared, Oliver. I want this baby so much.'

'Me, too,' he said. More than that, he wanted Ella as well. Whatever had caused her to back off from him since the party, they could fix it—because she was more important to him than anything or anyone else. 'It's going to be OK, Ella. I promise you.'

She was crying silently, and he hated the fact that he couldn't do anything more to help; but, at the same time, he needed to get her to hospital safely.

It seemed to take for ever to get to Teddy's, even though he knew it couldn't have been more than twenty minutes. But at last they were there and he parked as close to the entrance as possible, then grabbed a wheelchair from the entrance.

'I can walk,' Ella protested.

'I know, but this is faster. Let me do this, Ella. Please. I won't smother you in cotton wool, but I want to get you in there for that scan.' His voice cracked and he wondered if she'd heard it and realised that he was as emotional about the situation as she was. And, actually, maybe she needed to know it. 'Not just for you. For me. I need to be sure you're both all right.'

He was almost breaking into a run by the time they got to Teddy's.

'Later,' he said to the nurse on the reception desk, who looked at Ella in shock as he wheeled her through. 'I'll explain later.'

Annabelle had texted him to say that Room Three was reserved for him, if she wasn't there when he brought Ella in. Oliver wheeled Ella into the room, scooped her out of the wheelchair and laid her on the bed. The fact that she made no protest this time really scared him.

'Can you bare your tummy—?' he began, but she was already doing it.

Please, please, let the baby be all right, he begged inwardly, and smeared the gel over her stomach.

His hands were actually shaking as he stroked the head of the transceiver across her abdomen.

But then he could see the little bean shape, and the heart was beating strongly.

Thank you, he said silently, and moved the screen so Ella could see it, too. 'Look,' he said. 'It's going to be OK. There's a really strong heart-beat, not too fast and not too slow. Everything's going to be fine, Ella.'

Her shoulders heaved, and then she was crying in earnest. He held her close, stroking her hair, and realised that tears were running down his cheeks, too.

He wanted this baby. So did she, desperately.

Surely there was a good chance that they could make a decent life together—the three of them, because now he realised how much he wanted that, too.

Finally Ella was all cried out—and then she realised that Oliver was still holding her. And she'd soaked his shirt. And was it her imagination, or were his eyes wet, too? She'd been so frightened that she hadn't been able to focus much on what he'd said to her, but had he said that he was scared, too?

She wasn't sure, and her first instinct was to back away in case she was making a fool of herself again. 'We ought to—well, someone else might need this room.'

'I want to admit you now and keep you in overnight,' he said, 'for observation.'

She shook her head. 'I'll be fine.'

'You're on bed-rest. Don't argue,' he said, 'and there's no way in hell you're working your shift today, so don't even suggest it.'

'But someone else might need the bed on the ward more than I do.'

'Ella, you're pregnant and you were in a car crash.'

'A minor crash. At low speed.'

'Bad enough that they had to get a tow-truck for your car,' he said. 'And you were spotting. If any of your mums came in presenting like that, what would you say?'

'Go home and rest,' she said, 'and come back if you're worried.'

'And if it was a mum you knew damn well didn't know the meaning of the word rest?'

'Then I'd suggest staying in,' she admitted.

'I know you think I'm wrapping you up in cotton wool,' he said, 'and I know that drives you mad—but what I don't get is why you won't let anyone look after you.'

'It's a long story,' she said.

He shrugged. 'I've got all the time in the world.'

He really expected her to tell him? Panic flooded through her. 'I don't know where to start.'

'Try the beginning,' he said. 'Or the middle— or anywhere that feels comfortable—and you can take it from there.'

She knew where to start, then. 'The baby. I didn't try to trap you.'

'I know. You're not Justine.'

She frowned. 'Justine?'

'It's a long story.'

What was sauce for the goose… 'I've got time,' she said. 'And maybe if you tell me, it'll give me the courage to tell you.'

He looked at her for a long moment, then finally nodded. 'OK. I'll go first. Justine was the daughter of my parents' friends. They'd kind of earmarked her for me as a suitable future wife, even though I wasn't ready to settle down and I wanted to get all my training out of the way first so I could qualify as an obstetrician. They fast-tracked me and I was just about to take my last exams when Justine told me she was pregnant.'

Ella went cold. So this wasn't the first time Oliver had been faced with an unexpected baby; it also went some way to explaining why Oliver's mother had been so disapproving about the baby, if the Countess had been in that position before. But as far as Ella knew Oliver didn't have a child. What had happened?

'I really wasn't ready to be a dad,' Oliver said.

'I'd been so focused on my studies. But I did the right thing and stood by her.'

'Like you're standing by me?' she couldn't help asking.

He didn't answer that, and she went colder still.

'So we found a nice flat, moved in together, and sorted out a room for the baby.'

Oliver definitely wouldn't have abandoned the baby. This must have ended in tragedy—or maybe Justine had refused him access to the baby and that was why the Countess had been adamant that Oliver should have custody.

His grey eyes were filled with pain and she squeezed his hand. Clearly the memories hurt him, and she didn't want that. 'You don't have to tell me anything more.'

'Yes, I do,' he said. 'I don't want there to be any more secrets between us. I should've told you about this a long time ago.' He dragged in a breath. 'We'd planned to get married after the baby was born. But then one day she accidentally picked up my phone instead of hers and went out. I assumed that the phone on the table was mine and was about to put it in my pocket when a text came through.' He grimaced. 'Obviously I didn't set out to spy on her and read her texts, because I trusted her, but the message came up on her lock screen and I read it before I realised it was a private message for her.' He looked away. 'It was from another man, and the wording made it clear they were having an affair. I tackled her about it when she got home and she admitted the baby was his, not mine.'

'So that's why—' She stopped abruptly. Now wasn't the time to tell him that his mother wanted her to have a paternity test.

'Why what?'

'Nothing. I'm so sorry, Oliver. That was a vile thing to do to you. But why would she lie to you like that?'

He shrugged. 'You've been to Darrington Hall and met my family. I guess it was the kind of lifestyle she wanted and the other guy couldn't give her that.'

Now Ella could understand his mother's comments about gold-diggers. But did Oliver think she was a gold-digger too—despite the fact that she'd told him she wasn't? He'd been in that situation before. And now she realised why he'd been so controlling with her when she'd told him about the baby, because Justine had taken all his choices away. Ella had reacted by being stubbornly independent, and they'd been at cross purposes when it needn't have been like that at all.

'It's still horrible for you. And not all women think like that, you know.'

'I know.' His fingers tightened round hers. 'You don't.'

She was relieved that he realised that. 'Was the—was the baby all right?'

'Yes. I moved out and the other guy moved in—but from what I hear it didn't last.'

And then a really horrible thought hit her. Was Oliver still in love with Justine? Was that why he couldn't move on? She didn't want to ask him, because she was too scared that the answer might be 'yes'.

As if he'd guessed at her thoughts, he said, 'You're not Justine, and I don't have a shred of doubt that this baby's mine. I'm just sorry I haven't been able to get my head round things properly and support you the way I should've done.'

Relief made her sag back against the bed. 'Now you've told me what happened to you before, I can understand why you reacted the way you did.'

'Though I did wonder if you were lying to me,' he said, 'when you said it was safe and I assumed you were on the Pill.'

'I thought it *was* safe,' Ella said. 'I honestly never thought I'd ever get pregnant.'

'That's what I don't understand. I haven't found the right way to ask you because...' He grimaced. 'Ella, I didn't want to fight with you over it. But, once you'd told me you were pregnant, I couldn't work out why you were so sure that I didn't need contraception and yet you weren't on the Pill. I knew there was something, but asking you straight out felt intrusive and as if I was accusing you of something, and I didn't want that.'

He'd been honest with her, so now she needed to be honest with him. At least she wouldn't have to explain the medical side too much because it was Oliver's speciality and he understood it. 'I have endometriosis. It caused a lot of scarring on my Fallopian tubes over the years, and then I had an ovarian cyst that ruptured during my training. The doctors in London told me that I was infertile.'

'So that's why you said I didn't...'

'...need a condom,' she finished. 'Yes.'

'I'm sorry. Endometriosis is pretty debilitating, and to get news like that when you're so young...'

'Yes.' She'd cried herself to sleep for weeks afterwards. 'Worse was that it disrupted my studies.'

'Didn't you tell your tutors? They would've understood.'

She grimaced. 'You've read my file, so you know I'm dyslexic.'

He nodded.

'I wasn't diagnosed with dyslexia until I was fifteen. Everyone just thought I was a bit slow because I had trouble reading and I'm clumsy. I was always the last to be picked for the netball team in PE lessons, because I could never catch a ball, and you really don't want to see me trying to throw one.' She shrugged. 'Anyway, the September I turned fifteen we all knew I wasn't going to do well over the next two years, so I wasn't going to get good grades in my exams. But I was good with people and had the gift of the gab, so everyone thought I ought to go and work in the local pub, at first in the kitchen and then in the bar when I was old enough.'

'Right.'

'Except I had a new science teacher that year, and she took me to one side after the first week and asked me all kinds of questions. She was the first teacher ever at school who seemed to think I wasn't slow.' And it had been so liberating. Suddenly it had been possible to dream. 'She said she thought I had dyslexia, because I was fine at answering questions on stuff we'd talked about in class but when she looked at my written work it wasn't anywhere near the same standard, and my writing was terrible. Nobody had ever tested me for dyslexia—they'd never even considered it. So my teacher talked to my parents and the Special Needs department at school and they got me tested.'

'And it turned out she was right?'

She nodded. 'They gave me coloured glasses and got my test papers printed on pastel colours instead of bright white, and suddenly bookwork wasn't quite so much of a struggle any more.' She smiled. 'I'd always wanted to be a midwife like my Aunty Bridget, but nobody ever thought I was clever enough to do it. But I got through my exams, I stayed on at sixth form and I actually got accepted at uni. I was already getting help for my dyslexia, because they let me record all my lectures to help me revise, so I didn't feel I could go to my tutors and say there was another problem as well. It felt like one excuse too many.'

Now Oliver began to understand why Ella was so independent. She'd had to fight hard to get where she was, and she'd no doubt been wrapped in cotton wool as the child who always under-achieved—as well as being told that she was stu-pid by people who should never have judged her in the first place.

'And I guess,' she said, 'there was a part of me that didn't want to admit it because then I'd have to admit I wasn't a real woman—that I'd never be able to give my partner a child of his own.'

'Ella, being infertile doesn't make you any less of a woman,' Oliver said.

'That's easy for you to say, being a man,' she said softly. 'I knew my parents were desperate for grandchildren and I'd let them down, too.'

'That's seriously what they believe?'

'No, of course not! They said it didn't matter if I didn't have children,' Ella said, 'but I've seen my mum's face whenever she talks about her great-nieces and great-nephews. Just for a second there's this wistfulness. She couldn't have any more children after me, so me not being able to have children meant that she'd never have grandchildren. So she and Da were thrilled to bits when I told them about the baby.'

Oliver was shocked. Hadn't they agreed to wait to tell their family until she'd got through the first trimester? 'You've told them already?'

'I'm sorry. I just couldn't wait,' she said simply. 'I know things are tricky for you with your parents, but mine aren't like that—they're so pleased.'

She'd thought she was infertile but, because of him, she was having a baby. It was almost like the Justine situation again except there wasn't any cheating, this time. Justine had wanted the lifestyle and not him. Did Ella want the baby and not him?

He shook himself. But he wanted this baby, too. And, before the Hallowe'en Masquerade Ball, he and Ella had been friends. So maybe they could make this work, the way it hadn't with Justine.

'My parents are dying to meet you,' Ella said.

'So do I need to ask your father officially for your hand in marriage?' Oliver asked.

She blinked at him. 'What?'

'It's the practical solution,' Oliver said. 'We both want this baby. We get along well, for the most part. So we'll get married and give the baby a stable home.'

We both want this baby... Get married... A stable home.

But Oliver hadn't said a word about love. Or actually *asked* her to marry him.

And all Ella could think of was what Sienna had said about it being better for a baby to have one parent who loved it to bits than two parents who fought all the time. Given the situation with Oliver's parents, there was a good chance that she and Oliver would fight. A lot.

Marrying her meant he'd get custody of the baby: exactly what his mother wanted.

Even though Ella understood now what might have driven the Countess to take that view, she also didn't want her life taken over by the Darringtons—to have to give her baby the name they chose, send the baby to the school they chose, and give up her job to take on the role they chose.

If Oliver had said one word to her about love, it would've been different.

But he hadn't. And she couldn't marry someone who didn't love her. It wouldn't be a real relationship. That wasn't what she wanted.

'No,' she said.

CHAPTER TEN

OLIVER STARED AT ELLA, not quite believing what he was hearing.

He'd proposed to her—and she'd refused.

'Why?' he asked.

'I'm not marrying you just for the baby's sake. And I'm perfectly happy for my baby to be an O'Brien.' Her expression was closed.

'But—this is my baby, too.' He looked at her, shocked. 'Or are you telling me…?'

She blew out a breath. 'Now I know what your ex did, I can understand why you're worrying that it's history repeating itself, but don't you know me better than that?'

He'd thought he knew her. But maybe he didn't. And maybe she did have one thing in common with Justine, then: her feelings for him weren't the same as his for her. 'I asked you to marry me.'

'For the baby's sake.' She swallowed hard. 'Like your mother—' She stopped abruptly.

'What about my mother?'

'Nothing.'

'It doesn't sound like nothing to me.'

'All right—if you must know,' Ella said, 'she wants the baby.'

'What?' He'd never heard anything more ridiculous in his life. His mother didn't even *know* about the baby.

'Provided you have a paternity test first to make quite sure it's yours,' Ella continued. 'And then you'll sue me for custody.'

This was getting more and more surreal. 'What? Why?'

'Because Darrington babies have a position to maintain.'

'That's ridiculous. Of course my mother wouldn't say anything like that,' Oliver said. 'And when did she say anything to you? I was with you nearly all the time at Darrington.'

'Not all the time. Not when I'd gone to splash my face with water.'

'You're saying my mother accosted you in the bathroom?' That definitely wasn't his mother's style.

'She'd been watching me and she'd worked out

that I was going green around the lilies. And I was the first person you'd brought there in years, so there was obviously a reason why you wanted them to meet me.'

Oliver shook his head, unable to take this in.

'Believe what you like,' she said. 'But I'm not marrying you.' She turned away.

Oliver raked a hand through his hair. What the hell was going on? 'Ella—'

'I could do with some rest,' she said.

Because she'd just had a car crash and a nasty scare about the baby. And she'd been here at the hospital all night, keeping Georgie company until Leo arrived from New York.

Of course she could do with some rest. She must be exhausted, physically and mentally and emotionally.

Maybe that was why she was flinging around these wild accusations—she was sleep-deprived and still worried sick about the baby, and saying the first thing that came into her head instead of thinking about it. Maybe if he gave her some space and some time to sleep, she'd get her head round things and talk this over sensibly with him.

'I'll arrange for you to be moved to a side room,' he said stiffly, and left the treatment room.

'Is everything OK?' Annabelle asked, coming over to him as he strode through the department.

'With the baby? Yes.'

She frowned. 'Is Ella all right?'

'She needs to be moved to a side room and kept in overnight for observation,' Oliver said. 'Excuse me.'

'Oliver—'

'Not now,' he said, and headed for his office. And for once he actually closed his door. Usually he was happy to be interrupted by any member of staff who needed him, but right now he needed to lose himself in paperwork and not have to deal with another human being.

He was halfway through a pile of admin when his phone buzzed; he glanced at the screen.

Darrington Hall.

Why were his parents calling him?

For a moment, he thought about just ignoring the call. But then again it might be important. With a sigh, he answered.

'Oliver. I was just checking if you were coming home for Christmas,' his mother said.

He nearly laughed. Darrington Hall hadn't been 'home' for a long, long time. 'I'm afraid not,' he said. 'I'm on duty.'

'Can't you change it?'

'No,' he said. But something was eating at him. Had his mother really had a fight with Ella outside the bathroom? He'd thought at the time that Ella had been gone a long while. And she'd been very cool with him after that. If his mother had just warned her off him, that would explain why she'd gone cold on him. 'Mama—did you tell Ella you wanted her to have a paternity test?'

'I... Why would I do that?'

He noticed that his mother hadn't denied all knowledge of Ella being pregnant. He was pretty sure that Ella wouldn't have volunteered the information willingly, the way she had with her own family. And he knew exactly what would've driven his mother to talk about a paternity test. 'Justine,' he said succinctly.

'Well, I don't want to see you trapped again.'

It was the nearest his mother would get to admitting what she'd said. 'Ella isn't trying to trap me,' Oliver said. She'd just refused to marry him. He paused. Now he thought about it, that stuff about Darrington babies having a position to maintain sounded just like the sort of thing his mother would say. 'What position does a Darrington baby have to maintain?'

'I don't know what you mean.'

That definitely sounded like bluster. 'Mother, I'm not the heir to Darrington.'

'You will be if Edward and Prudence don't get their skates on and produce a boy.'

He let that pass. 'And, for the record, I have no intention of suing Ella for custody.'

'Custody?'

'Yes. Did you tell her we wanted custody? Because Darrington babies have a position to maintain?' he repeated.

'I—Oliver, you know it would be for the best. We could hire a nanny. There's plenty of space here—'

'No,' he cut in. 'Ella is the mother of my child, and the baby stays with her.'

'I see.' His mother's tone became frosty.

He sighed. 'Mama, I know we don't see eye-to-eye about my job. But I've been either a medical student or a qualified doctor for seventeen years now. Half a lifetime, almost. I'm not going to change my mind about what I do. And you need to start trusting me, because I'm doing what's right for me.'

'But, Oliver, Ella's—'

'Ella's lovely,' he said, 'as you'd know if you actually gave her a chance, the way Ned and Prue did. Think about it. Yes, things went wrong with Justine. On paper she was the perfect match, and you pushed us together—and it went wrong. This time, I'm making my own choice. I don't care if Ella's parents don't have the same pedigree that you do. It doesn't matter where you come from, Mama—what matters is who you are and how you treat other people.'

And he hadn't treated Ella very kindly just now.

'I'm going to be a father,' he said quietly. 'And I'd like my baby to know both sets of grandparents. Properly. I'd like to build some bridges with you and Papa. But in turn you need to respect that I'm old enough and wise enough to make my own decisions.'

'And your own mistakes?' the Countess asked coldly.

'Ella isn't a mistake,' he said. 'And neither is my career.'

'So you're giving me an ultimatum?'

'No. I'm giving you a chance to get to know the woman I love, and our baby,' he said. 'It's not going to happen overnight and we're all going to have to learn to compromise a bit, but I guess that's part of what being a real family means.'

'Oliver...'

'I'm on leave at New Year,' he said. 'Maybe we could start with lunch. Something small, informal and friendly. Just you, Papa, Ned and Prue and the girls, and us. Nobody else. Just family. You can get to know Ella a bit better—and we'll take it from there.'

'Just family, New Year,' the Countess echoed.

'A new year and a new beginning,' he said softly.

For a long time, she said nothing, and he thought she was going to throw it all back in his face.

But then she sighed. 'All right.'

'Good. I'll speak to you soon,' he said.

But, more importantly, he needed to talk to Ella. To apologise for ever having doubted her. He wasn't going to take her an armful of flowers—apart from the fact that there was a ban on flowers while the vomiting bug was still around, flowers weren't going to fix things. The only way to fix things was by total honesty.

He just hoped that she'd hear him out.

When he went back onto the ward, Annabelle was there. 'Which room is Ella in?' he asked.

'I'm not entirely sure I should tell you,' she said, narrowing her eyes at him. 'At the moment, Oliver Darrington, I'd quite like to shake you until your teeth rattle.'

He blinked, not used to his head nurse being so fierce. 'What have I done?'

She scoffed. 'Are you really that dense? You made Ella cry.'

He winced. 'I need to talk to her.'

'You need,' Annabelle said crisply, 'to grovel.'

'That, too,' he said.

'She's in here.' Annabelle indicated the side room. 'But if you make her cry any more, I'll throw you out personally, and I don't care if you're the Assistant Head of Obstetrics.'

'You won't have to do that,' Oliver said.

'Hmm,' Annabelle said, and watched him as he walked into the room.

He closed the door behind him, noting that Ella was in tears.

'Hey,' he said softly.

She looked at him and scrubbed at her eyes with the back of one hand. 'What do you want?'

'To talk. To apologise.' He paused. 'Annabelle says I need to grovel.'

Ella's face was tight. 'It doesn't matter.'

'Why are you crying?'

'It doesn't matter,' she repeated.

'Yes, it does,' he said. 'Are you crying because I walked out?'

She didn't answer.

'Because, earlier,' he said, 'you seemed to think that me walking out on you would make you happy. What do you want, Ella?'

'Something you can't give me,' she said. 'You don't do relationships. I was stupid to think that maybe I could change your mind on that score, especially now I know why you don't date anyone more than twice.'

'But that's what I want, too,' he said, coming to sit beside her. 'I want a proper relationship. I want to be a proper family. With you.'

'Your family will never accept me,' she said.

'Your brother and Prue are nice, but your mum hates me and your dad despises me, so it's never going to work. It's just going to cause endless rows between you and them, and that's going to make things difficult between you and me.'

'My parents,' he said, 'are difficult, but they're going to learn to change. And I'm sorry that my mother harangued you outside the bathroom and said I'd insist on custody after a paternity test.'

She frowned. 'But you said she wouldn't say things like that.'

'I didn't want to think she'd say it,' he said, 'but what you said rang pretty true. Oh, and she's sorry, by the way.'

Ella stared at him, looking surprised. 'You've spoken to your mother?'

'Technically, she rang me,' he said. 'So I asked her about what she'd said to you. And I told her very bluntly that you're the mother of my child and the baby stays with you.'

'So you're not going to sue me for custody?'

'I was rather hoping,' he said, 'that we could do better than that. That we could be a family.'

She shook her head. 'I'm not marrying you for the baby's sake, Oliver. That won't work, either.

We'll end up resenting each other and it won't be good for the baby.'

'That isn't why I asked you, actually,' he said. 'I asked you because I want to marry you for you. Because I love you.'

She scoffed. 'We had a one-night stand with consequences neither of us was expecting. That's not love, Oliver.'

'Agreed, but that's got nothing to do with it. I've known you for eighteen months,' he said. 'The first moment I saw you, I noticed you. That glorious hair, those beautiful eyes, and a mouth that made my knees weak.'

She looked stunned.

'And then I got to know this bright, warm midwife who's a joy to work with,' Oliver continued. 'She's great with the mums and makes them all feel a million times better when they're panicking, she's great at explaining things to our trainees and gives them confidence when they don't think they can do things, and she thinks on her feet so she can second-guess what senior staff need, too—and I admit, that's why I didn't ask you out months ago, because I know I'm rubbish at relationships and I didn't want to mess up things at work. But then it was the night of the ball—and yes, I'm shallow, because it's the first time I saw you all dressed up and I couldn't think straight. Especially when I danced with you. I wanted to go and reclaim you from every other guy you danced with,' he told her.

'Really?'

'Really,' he confirmed. 'I couldn't resist you. And then it got complicated, because I realised what I'd done, and I'd messed everything up, and I didn't know how to make things right between us again.'

'And then I told you about the baby—and that must've brought back memories of Justine,' she said quietly.

'It did, though I never doubted you for a second and I don't want you to do a paternity test. The night of the party, when you made me feel you really believed in me and supported me— I've never had that from anyone before. It threw me. And it made me realise that maybe you were the one I could trust with my heart. Except then you started avoiding me, and when I asked you to marry me you said no.'

'Because you never said a word about your feelings,' she said. 'I thought you were asking me to marry you out of duty, just because you thought it was the right thing to do. You said we got on well and we could give the baby a stable home—but that's not enough, Oliver. You need love as well, to make a family.'

'I'm not very good at talking about my feelings,' he said. 'But I do love you, Ella. And I do want to be a family with you and the baby. Not like the way I grew up, with my parents very distant and leaving most of the care to hired staff. I want to take the baby to the park with you, and feed the ducks together, and read bedtime stories, and be there in the playground on the first day our little one starts school.'

'The local school?' she checked.

'Definitely the local school,' he said. 'I want to be a family with you and our baby.'

He meant it, Ella realised.

Oliver really did love her. He wanted to make a life with her and the baby—not because he thought it was the right thing to do, but because he *wanted* to be with them. That day on the ward when he'd talked about taking their baby to see

Santa: that had been the real Oliver. The hidden Oliver.

Ella felt her heart contract sharply. 'I love you, too, Oliver,' she said. 'I fell for you months ago.'

'But you never said anything.'

'I thought I was out of your league,' she said. 'The hospital rumour mill said you only ever dated supermodels.'

He laughed. 'Hardly. Anyway, you could hold your own against any supermodel.'

'I'm too short and too curvy,' she said.

'No way. You're beautiful,' he said. 'And I don't want a supermodel. I want you. I love you.'

She stroked his face. 'I love you, too.'

'Even though I'm a grumpy control freak?'

'Even though you're a grumpy control freak,' she said. 'And I guess that's why I called you today when I started bleeding, because I trust you and I knew you'd be there for me. Just as I hope you know I'll always be there for you.'

'Then I'll ask you the same question I asked earlier, except this time I'll do it properly.' He knelt down on one knee. 'Ella O'Brien, you're the love of my life and I want to make a family with you—will you marry me?'

And this time she knew he meant it. That this was going to be a real marriage, not papering over the cracks. 'Yes.'

There was a rap on the door and Annabelle came in. She frowned as she took in the tears on Ella's face. 'Oliver Darrington, I warned you not to make Ella cry,' she said, putting her hands on her hips. 'And you didn't listen. So that's it. *Out.*'

'Annabelle, I'm not crying because I'm miserable,' Ella said, hastily. 'I'm crying because I'm happy.'

Annabelle looked confused. 'So he grovelled?'

'I probably still need to do a bit more grovelling,' Oliver admitted, 'but we're getting there—and we're looking for a matron of honour. I don't suppose you know anyone who might be up for the job? Someone, say, in this room?'

Annabelle's jaw dropped and she stared at each of them in turn. 'You're getting married?'

'You're the first to know,' Ella said. 'Would you be our matron of honour?'

'And godmother to Baby Darrington?' Oliver added.

Annabelle smiled. 'Absolutely yes. To both.'

EPILOGUE

A year later

'BA-BA! DA-DA!' five-month-old Harry crowed, waving his chubby little hands as his father walked into the living room.

'Hello, Harrykins.' Oliver swept his son up into his arms and gave him a resounding kiss. 'Have you been good for Mummy today?'

'Ba-ba,' Harry said solemnly.

'I'm glad to hear it.' Oliver blew a raspberry on the baby's cheek, making him giggle, and put him back in his bouncy chair.

'And good afternoon to you, Mrs Darrington,' he said, taking Ella into his arms and kissing her. 'Guess what I managed to borrow today?'

'Reindeer? Sleigh? A snow machine?'

'Not far off,' he said. 'Wait. Close your eyes. And no peeking.'

Ella smiled and followed his directions.

'OK. You can look now,' he said. 'Ho-ho-ho.'

She burst out laughing, seeing him wearing the Santa outfit from the ward.

Harry, on the other hand, took one look at the strange man in the red hooded suit and white beard, and burst into tears.

Swiftly, Oliver pulled the hood back and removed the beard. 'Harrykins, it's all right. It's Daddy.' He looked at Ella. 'Sorry. I had no idea it'd scare him like this.'

'He's still only five months old and he doesn't really know what's going on. Next Christmas,' she said, 'he'll be old enough to appreciate it and you'll get the reaction you were expecting today.' She scooped the baby into her arms and rocked him gently. 'Harry, it's OK. It really *is* Daddy.'

Harry simply screamed.

Thirty seconds later, the doorbell went.

'I'll go,' Oliver said.

'Oliver Darrington, why are you half dressed as Father Christmas?' the Countess of Darrington asked in crisp tones on the doorstep. 'And why is my grandson wailing like that?'

'Those two things are connected, and I'm an

idiot,' Oliver said. 'Hello, Mama. I didn't realise you were coming over tonight.'

'Your father and I just collected Joe and Roisin from the airport,' Catherine said. 'Or had you forgotten they were coming?'

'He was too excited about being Harry's very first Father Christmas to remember that you're all going to be here for dinner tonight,' Ella said with a grin, walking into the doorway with a still-sobbing Harry. 'And you need to take that suit off, Oliver, and hide it before Prue, Ned and the children get here, because the girls are still young enough to believe in Santa and I don't want to spoil it for them.'

'Tsk. Go and sort yourself out, Oliver. Give the boy to me,' Catherine said, holding out her arms, and Ella duly handed over the baby. 'There, there, Harry. Nobody's going to scare you when Granny Darrington's around.'

Probably, Oliver thought, because his mother was the scariest thing around.

Two seconds later, Harry stopped crying and started gurgling at his grandmother.

And Oliver couldn't quite be annoyed that his

mother seemed to have a knack for soothing the baby, because it was so nice to see his family all on such good terms.

'I'll put the kettle on,' Ella said. 'Catherine, I bought some of that horrible lapsang souchong you like, this morning.'

'Thank you, my dear,' Catherine said.

'And there's some good proper tea for me, I hope,' Roisin chipped in, walking into the hallway and overhearing the conversation.

'Of course, Mum.' Ella kissed her mother warmly.

'Your turn for a cuddle, Roisin,' Catherine said, handing over the baby. 'And I'll make the tea, Ella. That baby's had you running round all day and you ought to put your feet up.'

Oliver hid a smile. If anyone had told him a year ago that the two most important women in his life would become fast friends, he would never have believed it. But he'd gradually rebuilt his relationship with his parents, starting with the quiet family lunch he'd suggested at New Year. Things had still been a little strained between them until one day when the baby had started kicking, and Ella had gone over to Catherine, taken her hand and placed it on the bump, saying, 'Baby Darrington, say hello to Granny Darrington.' Catherine had been rewarded by some very firm kicks, and from that point on she'd warmed to Ella.

The O'Briens had instantly adopted Oliver as one of their own and, although Oliver had been wary about the first meeting between Roisin and Catherine, to his surprise they'd got on really well. Roisin was too straightforward for there to be any misunderstandings; and, once Catherine had discovered just how well Roisin played the piano, they'd bonded over a shared love of music and their future grandbaby.

Prue and Ned had also had a son, a couple of weeks before Ella had Harry, so Oliver was no longer the 'spare'. To his delight, having that pressure taken off meant that his parents had finally accepted what he did for a living. Catherine had even suggested that the next Darrington Christmas cocktail party should be a fundraiser for Teddy's. She'd been backed by Ella, Prue and Roisin; and the O'Briens had come over from

Ireland this week to help with the last-minute arrangements for the party.

Life, Oliver thought, didn't get any better than this.

Knowing that his father and Joe were bringing in the luggage, and Catherine and Roisin were in the kitchen with the baby, he scooped Ella into his arms and swung her round before kissing her. 'Hey. Happy Christmas. I love you.'

She kissed him back. 'Happy Christmas, Oliver. I love you, too.' She smiled. 'I thought last year I had the best present ever, when I found out that I was expecting our Harry, but I was wrong. Because this is the best present ever—our family, all together.'

'Our family, all together,' he agreed, and kissed her again.

* * * * *

If you missed the first story in the
CHRISTMAS MIRACLES IN MATERNITY
quartet look out for

THE NURSE'S CHRISTMAS GIFT
by Tina Beckett

And there are two more fabulous
stories to come!

If you enjoyed this story,
check out these other great reads
from Kate Hardy

CAPTURING THE SINGLE DAD'S HEART
HER PLAYBOY'S PROPOSAL

MILLS & BOON®
Large Print Medical

June

White Christmas for the Single Mum	Susanne Hampton
A Royal Baby for Christmas	Scarlet Wilson
Playboy on Her Christmas List	Carol Marinelli
The Army Doc's Baby Bombshell	Sue MacKay
The Doctor's Sleigh Bell Proposal	Susan Carlisle
Christmas with the Single Dad	Louisa Heaton

July

Falling for Her Wounded Hero	Marion Lennox
The Surgeon's Baby Surprise	Charlotte Hawkes
Santiago's Convenient Fiancée	Annie O'Neil
Alejandro's Sexy Secret	Amy Ruttan
The Doctor's Diamond Proposal	Annie Claydon
Weekend with the Best Man	Leah Martyn

August

Their Meant-to-Be Baby	Caroline Anderson
A Mummy for His Baby	Molly Evans
Rafael's One Night Bombshell	Tina Beckett
Dante's Shock Proposal	Amalie Berlin
A Forever Family for the Army Doc	Meredith Webber
The Nurse and the Single Dad	Dianne Drake

MILLS & BOON®
Large Print Medical

September

Their Secret Royal Baby	Carol Marinelli
Her Hot Highland Doc	Annie O'Neil
His Pregnant Royal Bride	Amy Ruttan
Baby Surprise for the Doctor Prince	Robin Gianna
Resisting Her Army Doc Rival	Sue MacKay
A Month to Marry the Midwife	Fiona McArthur

October

Their One Night Baby	Carol Marinelli
Forbidden to the Playboy Surgeon	Fiona Lowe
A Mother to Make a Family	Emily Forbes
The Nurse's Baby Secret	Janice Lynn
The Boss Who Stole Her Heart	Jennifer Taylor
Reunited by Their Pregnancy Surprise	Louisa Heaton

November

Mummy, Nurse...Duchess?	Kate Hardy
Falling for the Foster Mum	Karin Baine
The Doctor and the Princess	Scarlet Wilson
Miracle for the Neurosurgeon	Lynne Marshall
English Rose for the Sicilian Doc	Annie Claydon
Engaged to the Doctor Sheikh	Meredith Webber

MILLS & BOON®
Large Print – June 2017

ROMANCE

The Last Di Sione Claims His Prize	Maisey Yates
Bought to Wear the Billionaire's Ring	Cathy Williams
The Desert King's Blackmailed Bride	Lynne Graham
Bride by Royal Decree	Caitlin Crews
The Consequence of His Vengeance	Jennie Lucas
The Sheikh's Secret Son	Maggie Cox
Acquired by Her Greek Boss	Chantelle Shaw
The Sheikh's Convenient Princess	Liz Fielding
The Unforgettable Spanish Tycoon	Christy McKellen
The Billionaire of Coral Bay	Nikki Logan
Her First-Date Honeymoon	Katrina Cudmore

HISTORICAL

The Harlot and the Sheikh	Marguerite Kaye
The Duke's Secret Heir	Sarah Mallory
Miss Bradshaw's Bought Betrothal	Virginia Heath
Sold to the Viking Warrior	Michelle Styles
A Marriage of Rogues	Margaret Moore

MEDICAL

White Christmas for the Single Mum	Susanne Hampton
A Royal Baby for Christmas	Scarlet Wilson
Playboy on Her Christmas List	Carol Marinelli
The Army Doc's Baby Bombshell	Sue MacKay
The Doctor's Sleigh Bell Proposal	Susan Carlisle
Christmas with the Single Dad	Louisa Heaton

0517 GEN STD LP

MILLS & BOON®

Why shop at millsandboon.co.uk?

Each year, thousands of romance readers find their perfect read at millsandboon.co.uk. That's because we're passionate about bringing you the very best romantic fiction. Here are some of the advantages of shopping at www.millsandboon.co.uk:

* **Get new books first**—you'll be able to buy your favourite books one month before they hit the shops

* **Get exclusive discounts**—you'll also be able to buy our specially created monthly collections, with up to 50% off the RRP

* **Find your favourite authors**—latest news, interviews and new releases for all your favourite authors and series on our website, plus ideas for what to try next

* **Join in**—once you've bought your favourite books, don't forget to register with us to rate, review and join in the discussions

Visit **www.millsandboon.co.uk**
for all this and more today!